Never Meant To Be

Stephen Seitz

Paperback ISBN 978-1-78092-453-3
ePub ISBN 978-1-78092-454-0
PDF ISBN 978-1-78092-455-7

Published in the UK by MX Publishing
335 Princess Park Manor, Royal Drive, London, N11 3GX
www.mxpublishing.com

Cover design by www.staunch.com

CHAPTER ONE

The words painted on the battered tin dispatch box read, "John H. Watson, M.D., late Indian Army."

"I assure you, Ms. Kenyon, I have no more idea than you why this should fall into your hands," said the young blondish attorney who pushed it toward her. "Yet my grandmother's will was quite clear."

"Mr. Lawrence, may I have the key, please?"

The box had to be at least a hundred years old, and it took several attempts before the key even fit, but eventually the rusty tumblers creaked over and the box opened. Inside were notebooks, photographs, medals, and an ancient yellow envelope with the name "Cynthia Kenyon" scrawled in very poor handwriting on the top.

"Ms. Kenyon?"

Cynthia tried to keep a nervous tremor out of her hands as a dozen questions flitted through her mind. She opened the envelope slowly, and two tickets fell out.

"They're for the science museum fundraiser tonight," she said. "How on earth is that possible?"

"Someone is going to great lengths to get your attention," said Lawrence. "If this is what I think it is, you have come into a great deal of money."

"What?"

The attorney opened one of the notebooks and read aloud, his voice rising with excitement:

"Mortimer narrative, H. questions:

"'Sir Chas. lay on his face, his arms out, his fingers dug into the ground, and his featrs. convulsd with some strong emotion to such an Xtent I could hardly swear to his ID. There was certainly no physical injury of any kind. But one false statement by Brymore at the inquest. He said no traces on the ground around the body. He did not observe any. But I did – some little distance off, but fresh and clear.

"'Footprints?

"'Footprints.

"'A man's or a woman's?

"Odd expr. on Mort. face.

"'Mr. Holmes, they were the footprints of a gigantic hound!'"

Cynthia, puzzled, asked, "Excuse me, Mr. Lawrence, but what was that?"

"It's an excerpt from *The Hound of the Baskervilles,* right from Doctor Watson's own notebook. All the notes for the cases of Sherlock Holmes are right in here. And for some reason, they're yours."

"I thought those stories were fiction."

"There's been some debate about that for years," Lawrence said. "I should add that I haven't been entirely honest with you."

"What?"

"You see, until recently, this box belonged to my grandmother, and here's what she told me.

"Dearest Leo,

"Kidnap her if you have to, but make certain that Cynthia Kenyon attends the science museum fundraiser at any cost. History depends on it.

"Love,

"Gran

"If you don't mind a total stranger being your date, I think we'll have some fun," Leo said.

Cynthia considered this. Leo Lawrence wore his suit well, she liked his wavy blond hair, and at least he had a good job. In her 27 years, she had done worse. It was only for one night, anyway.

"How do I dress for it?"

"The theme is the new exhibit which opens to the public on Saturday, 'Science in the Victorian Era.' Perfect for that Victorian party dress you've been wondering what to do with."

"I'm afraid I'll have to stay in this century, if it's all the same to you."

"Your best judgment should be fine. Pick you up at seven-thirty? There will be a few speeches, some dancing to the music of the time, and you'll get to see the exhibit before the rest of the world. My idea of a great evening, actually. Also, you can call me Leo."

"All right, Leo. I'm Cynthia. Not Cindy, let me make that clear. I live in the Charlestown Towers second building. Just buzz number 441 when you get there."

Leo gave her a warm and friendly smile.

"I'll see you then," he said. "In the meantime, this is going into our vault for safekeeping. Once word gets out, you'll never hear the end of it."

The Acoreus Museum of Science and Astronomy held pride of place in the city, sitting atop its highest hill and protected from the city lights by an elaborate arrangement of trees and buildings which framed its famous telescope. Four other buildings in neo-Classical style completed the museum complex: the agriculture and environmental sciences building; the botanical garden; computer science; and the history of technology building, where the new Victorian science exhibit would soon open.

Cynthia felt a little out of place among the bustles and frock coats some visitors wore, while she had donned a shimmering white satin blouse with a cowl neck, black skirt and matching pumps, and found herself having a very good time. Leo Lawrence proved a good dance partner, the food a plethora of Victorian culinary delights – triangular tea sandwiches filled with smoked salmon or watercress, cucumber sandwiches as well, lemon scones, lemon kisses, and plum puffs. A small orchestra played surprisingly enjoyable light music from the 1880s and

1890s, including some well-remembered tunes from Gilbert and Sullivan.

"Enjoying yourself?"

"Leo, I'm amazed to say I am. I never get to attend things like this."

"Really? Too busy, I'd guess. Dance card always full, right?"

Cynthia laughed, tossing her chestnut hair, and replied, "Steadily single city girl. My nights are filled with TV, Chablis, and stupid arguments on Facebook. The pathetic reality of a copyeditor's life."

"I'm beginning to think I might want to change that," he said.

When the music ended, a couple of museum luminaries made some introductory speeches, including the technology museum's director, Dr. April Cape.

"Wow, this gig pays," Cynthia whispered. "Those shoes alone amount to a car payment for me."

Cynthia placed the woman's age somewhere between 44 and 48, and her body showed signs of a woman trying to regain her figure; from her own experience, Cynthia recognized the signs of a recent return to the gym in Dr. Cape's glowing red cheeks and wet spots from a shower finished probably not more than an hour before. She had to admire the older woman's lightly streaked auburn hair, which framed her best feature, the radiant, penetrating blue eyes.

"Thank you all for your support in our latest endeavor, 'Science in the Victorian Era: Path to the Future,'" she said. "In this exhibit, you will see both the inventions which anticipated everyday items in our lives today, some which might have been, and the products of true geniuses whose creative vision would and could never be realized. I know I could bore you with more, but I won't. Feel free to ask any of the docents or myself any questions you may have. And, again, thank you for your generous support of the Acoreus Museum!"

With that, Dr. Cape stepped aside, and a member of the city council said a few words, after which the exhibit hall was opened.

The Victorian Era coincided with the Industrial Revolution and the rise of the middle class, which meant that most modern gadgets had their origin in the 19th century. The British were pioneers in steamships and communications. Cynthia was surprised to learn that primitive fax machines existed as far back as the 1840s. The Victorians in England had perfected the use of the telegraph, and that display included several famous ones, including a few from the early 20th century.

The text read: "To Dr. John Watson. Come at once if convenient. If inconvenient, come all the same. S.H."

"Sherlock Holmes," Leo said. "'The Adventure of the Creeping Man.' That connection again. Are you telling me you never read any of those stories?"

"Just a few in high school."

Cynthia found herself fascinated. Like so many people, to her history was just a series of dates and events you had to regurgitate in school. But on display here: the photographs of Muybridge and how his work photographing horses led to the development of cinema; specimens collected by Charles Darwin; how the first planned community, Saltaire, led to modern land use practices, and, of course, the centerpiece, advances in astronomy.

"Cynthia, take a look at this," said Leo. "It's got to be the reason Gran wanted you here."

Leo stood before a strange contraption, which looked like an enclosed sleigh. Designed to seat two in comfort, the dashboard had several labeled levers, but also a modern computerized dashboard and an LCD display. A large round disc in the back looked like some early form of solar battery.

"H.G.Wells' time machine, right?" Cynthia said.

She saw two men in oval sepia photographs on an explanatory plaque: one a photo of the younger H.G. Wells, circa 1890, and the other a bald, clean-shaven man whose sunken eyes and reptilian manner unsettled her somewhat.

The plaque read:

"H.G. Wells and Prof. James Moriarty

"While Prof. Moriarty is best remembered today as the nemesis of Sherlock Holmes, he was a widely respected mathematician before that. His treatise on the binomial theorem was highly advanced for its day, and his *Dynamics of an Asteroid* is still consulted by astronomers.

"Less well known are Moriarty's theories of time travel, titled *On the Nature of Time and Space,* in which Moriarty argued that time travel was mathematically possible, and also that slips in the time stream could be predicted and exploited.

"The book ended Moriarty's academic career. Though disdained my Moriarty's colleagues, *On the Nature of Time and Space* was embraced by one influential reader: H.G. Wells. Moriarty's theories resulted in Wells' famous novel, *The Time Machine.* Wells even went so far as to design a working model. The full scale model you see here was inspired by Wells' own plans.

"Based on H.G. Wells drawings and adapted by Roland Munson, Kenyon Scholar in residence."

"What?" Cynthia said. "I've never heard of that!"

"Curioser and curioser. I wonder if it works?" Leo said, as Cynthia folded a pamphlet explaining things further and stuffed it into her purse. She withdrew her cell phone and took some pictures.

Commotion reached their ears. Something was happening. Turning around, they saw two men wearing ski masks and brandishing pistols.

"Just put your money and jewelry into the duffel bag and nobody gets hurt," said one. "Everyone line up against the wall. Now!"

Leo set his jaw and pulled out his cell phone.

"Hey! I saw that!" snapped one, and he pointed his pistol at Leo.

He motioned Cynthia and Leo over to the wall where his partner was collecting valuables from the others. Leo moved in front of Cynthia.

"Leo, just do what the man says."

"My grandmother couldn't have known this would happen," he said. "She'd never do this to me."

A loud *crack!* and a bullet flew over Leo's head, triggering an alarm. That's when Leo rushed the bandit.

"You stupid—"the other thug yelled, which distracted his attention long enough for one of the other guests to tackle him. Cynthia saw a melee brewing, and she looked around. The exit was too far away, and she heard another shot as guards raced into the hall. Panicking, she stepped under the velvet cordon rope and into the time machine. She closed the door, crouching down.

She did not remember exactly what happened next. All light vanished. She had a strange sense of movement, but could not tell what was moving. She rose and sat, looking around, the darkness so complete it frightened her. She pulled her cell phone from her purse and took a flash photo, which revealed the dashboard and the numbers 06071882 on a red liquid crystal display, barely visible. She spotted some sort of lever. Desperate, she felt her way along the dashboard until she found the lever and yanked it toward her.

Nothing.

Cynthia leaned back and closed her eyes. The moving sensation gradually diminished. Strange smells reached her nostrils, horse manure the most prevalent, and the mustiness of a basement. The ambient noise seemed different, too: No small electric motors running, no sounds of ventilation, no buzzing from radios or TV.

Gradually, Cynthia understood that the sounds she heard came from nearby machinery and she caught the slight acrid stench of cleaning fluid. Emerging cautiously from the time machine, she found herself in a storage room full of crates containing machine parts, sheets of metal, chemicals and solvents. Following the noise to the next room, she saw two men working a machine that seemed to be stamping what looked at first glance to be metal bottle caps. She couldn't identify the source of light; they seemed to be using lanterns.

One of them, dressed like some sort of dusty workman, looked up and said in a thick London accent, "Christ Almighty! Who the hell are you? How'd you get in here?"

"I'm sorry," she said. "I don't know how I got in. I don't even know where I am!"

The other man, younger, also British and a bit cleaner, said, "You're American, eh? You sound American. But your clothing is so strange."

The men's blatant and frank appraisal of her appearance made Cynthia uncomfortable and she wanted to run. Who were these guys?

"I'm Cynthia Kenyon. Yes, I'm American. Please tell me where I am."

"In London, ma'am."

"Hold on, George. Ma'am, do you know what we're doing here?"

"It looks like you're making bottle caps. I can't tell in this light."

"That's it," said the other one. "That's exactly what we're doing. Why don't you go upstairs and wait for us in the parlor? We'll be finished here soon."

Cynthia felt for a light switch and found none. She made her way up to the basement door, and stepped into a kitchen that could have been her great-grandmother's. A large wood-fired black metal oven on four squat legs took up half of one wall. No refrigerator, but a dark loaf of bread and cheese lay on the sideboard, which reminded Cynthia she was hungry. She sliced a piece and went into the next room, which looked like a set for a Victorian costume drama: tables covered with lace, gas lamps, books, no sound system or TV. Cynthia took her cell phone from her small purse and tried to get a signal. No luck.

Can this be for real? she thought as fear began to settle in. *Where am I? When am I?*

Voices from the stairwell.

"Who the hell is she?" asked the one called George.

11

"We'd better ask the Professor. That looks like one of his contraptions in the storage room. Maybe she passed out in it and the Prof forgot about her."

"I'm sure Madam Marina has some work for her," said George and guffawed. "You look like you want to be first in line, Harry."

I don't like the sound of that, Cynthia thought. *Older one is Harry, younger one is George.*

"Ma'am? Where are you?"

"In here. I helped myself to a slice of bread. I hope you don't mind."

The men sat as daintily as they could on the chairs, telling Cynthia that neither of them lived there and they had respect for whoever did.

"I couldn't help overhearing you on the stairs," she said. "You mentioned the Professor. Would that be Professor Moriarty?"

Expressions of shock and fear as the men exchanged a glance.

"How do you know that?" demanded Harry. "Nobody's supposed to know that!"

"He's a famous mathematician," Cynthia said quickly. "Tall, bald, beady eyes, right?"

"Were you a student or something?"

"I attended some of his lectures, yes."

"Which school?"

"Oxford." *Here's where all that British TV pays off, I hope.*

"I don't like this, George. We'd better get her to the Prof straightaway."

"What? Why? I don't know anything!"

"But you sound like you know everything, and that's dangerous, girlie." Harry grabbed Cynthia's arm and squeezed, his grip firm. He nodded at George to grab the other arm.

"Into the basement until somebody gets here. And you'll need better answers for the Professor than for us."

That's when Cynthia kicked Harry hard in the knee and wrested her arm free from George.

"I need to see him anyway, but not as anyone's prisoner," she said. "He's partly responsible for bringing me here, and I need him to get back. I won't tell anybody about your machine shop. I don't care what you're doing down there. I just want to go home."

The men regarded her warily.

"For all you know, Professor Moriarty might be pretty angry for mistreating me," Cynthia said. "Do you want to take that chance?"

They shook their heads.

"Then you won't mind my waiting for him in the parlor."

"That won't do, ma'am. We'll have to take you to him."

"Please take care of it," she said. "I'm sorry if I upset you. I had no intention of coming here, and I have nothing to gain by ratting you out."

13

"Thank you, ma'am," Harry said. "I'm sorry for any misunderstanding."

As she waited, Cynthia found a newspaper. According to it, the date was July 7, 1882 or thereabouts. As she scanned the tightly packed columns of print, Cynthia felt her stomach clench as she realized the enormity of her position: no one she knew had even been born yet. She had credit cards and maybe $20 in cash, no clothes, nowhere to turn except to one of the most notorious criminal masterminds in modern history. An evil man who almost certainly wouldn't believe her.

An enclosed four-wheeled carriage Cynthia remembered from a long ago museum trip (now far in the future!) pulled up in front of the brownstone building. Harry and George escorted her to it.

"I certainly hope this is as important as you two make it sound," came a thin, reedy voice from inside. "You know the schedule."

"Professor, I think you're going to want to hear what this lady has to say," said George.

The door opened, and, her heart beginning to race, Cynthia stepped into the dark interior. In it sat a tall, thin man with sunken eyes and a nervous demeanor, his scalp bare. He had a nervous habit of turning his head a little from side to side, as if compensating for poor peripheral vision.

Next to him sat a burly man with a billy club.

"You are wearing the strangest clothes, and you get no commendations for modesty, Miss—"

"Kenyon, Cynthia Kenyon. It is truly an honor to meet you, Professor."

"How did you find me? Why do you seek me?"

Cynthia sat back for a moment and thought, *How do I tell him?*

"You won't easily believe what I have to say, but I have to ask: have you given any thought to the problem of time travel?"

Moriarty's eyes darkened with anger.

"You dare mention that fiasco to me? The paper that cost me my chair in mathematics? My greatest disgrace? I should fling you from the growler this instant!"

Cynthia shrank back and cried, "I'm the proof! You were right!"

Now his eyes went wide.

"How is that possible?" he demanded.

Cynthia told him of her night at the Acoreus museum, now decades away and yet only a few short hours ago.

"Someone built a machine?"

"H.G. Wells? Have you heard of him?"

Moriarty shook his head. Cynthia started to pull her cell phone from the purse, and stopped. There would be no signal, of course.

"That device. May I examine it, please?"

Cynthia handed it over.

15

"Please be careful. I need that," she said.

The professor gave the device a careful examination before handing it back and asking, "What does it do?"

"Many things," said Cynthia. "Let me show you one of them."

She secretly enjoyed the look on Professor Moriarty's face when the cell phone played its introductory electronic tones. After pressing some buttons, she turned the screen to Moriarty.

"These are photographs!" he exclaimed. "What colors!"

Cynthia changed the images: a party with friends, her father mugging for the camera from behind the wheel of the sports car he was finally able to afford, and some pictures from her weekend at Virginia Beach.

"Do you believe me now?" she asked.

"All this is in the future?"

"Yes. It's where I belong. I was hoping you could help me do that. The machine is back at the house where you picked me up. It's in the basement."

Moriarty's face darkened again.

"What did you see down there?"

"Some sort of metal stamping machine, but what they were making, I have no idea."

"I must give this some thought," he said.

"There's nothing to think about," she said. "I don't belong here. I have no money, no friends, no family. I know next to nothing about this time or place. What good does it do to keep me here?"

"The 21st century. I am known then?"

Cynthia almost told him the main reason, but said, "I am the vindication of your theory, Professor. They're still reading about the binomial theorem, and your *Dynamics of an Asteroid* is considered to be far ahead of its time."

"Will any of this be known in my lifetime?"

"Yes. Modern astronomers still look to your work. One of the reasons I'm here is that your work is on display in a major museum back home."

Moriarty thought some more and finally said, "I'm afraid my schedule is too full to deal with the matter today. I ask you to be my guest tonight. I can find you some more appropriate clothing, and I wish to know more about that strange device of yours."

Cynthia nodded, having no other choice.

"Good," the professor said.

CHAPTER TWO

Cynthia woke up when the door to her room opened and two pretty women about her age entered. She was surprised at how well she had slept, and how comfortable she felt in the simple white nightgown they had given her.

"Begging your pardon, miss," said the taller one, a blonde who gave her name as May, "but the professor sent us to show you how to dress."

"Where are my clothes?"

"Being laundered."

"My purse?"

Bridget, the shorter one, whose ginger hair marked her as Irish, handed it to her. Cynthia looked inside. Cell phone, keys, a wallet containing loose change, a twenty-dollar bill, her driver's license and her credit cards. She found her pen, the envelope with her tickets, all were there. The only thing missing was the pamphlet from the time machine exhibit.

"What am I to wear?"

"Not to worry, miss," said the blonde, who opened a dresser full of what Cynthia assumed was what women were wearing in London in 1882.

If the fashion industry of the 21st century treated women badly, it had nothing on the Victorians. First, black stockings, held up by garters, followed by cotton drawers. Then the women pulled a corset out.

"No," Cynthia said. "No way."

"You don't have a choice, miss. The professor insists—"

"Please tell the professor otherwise."

Genuine shock on the servants' faces.

"You do not ever say no to Professor Moriarty!" Bridget cried.

Feeling a bit nervous now, Cynthia assented.

"How do you breathe in this thing?" she said through gritted teeth as Bridget and May pulled the strings ever tighter.

"You've got to have a slender waist in this world, miss. I know you Americans do things differently, but—"

"Enough! Please!"

"Very good, miss."

Next layer, a camisole and petticoat to protect Cynthia's skin from what was coming next: the steel hoops, followed by a high-necked and long-sleeved, and most elaborate, blue dress. The shoes, surprisingly, proved quite comfortable, despite the square toes. Cynthia pinned her own hair up.

"The professor is waiting for you in the dining room," Bridget said. "Breakfast will be served shortly."

Notorious criminal mastermind he might be, but Cynthia found he set a splendid breakfast table: French pastries, fresh fruit, toast and marmalade, ham, bacon, scrambled eggs, coffee and tea. To Cynthia, who seldom had more than a slice of toast and a cup of coffee with milk in the morning, it seemed sumptuous.

19

"I see why women in this time period have to wear corsets," she said. "May I?"

Moriarty nodded, and Cynthia helped herself to pastries and fruit.

"You seem to have withheld some important information from me," he said.

"Professor, I don't understand."

Moriarty placed the museum pamphlet on the table.

"According to this, I am the Napoleon of crime, and I have but nine years to live," he said. "Who is Sherlock Holmes?"

Cynthia blanched.

"I—I—don't know," she said.

"Have you been sent to spy on me? Is this some sort of elaborate confidence scheme? Answer me!"

Two large, square and burly men stepped in from the next room.

"Professor, you saw my cell phone. How could I have faked that with Victorian technology? You examined my driver's license and my money, all of which are dated far in the future! I'm not lying!"

Moriarty regarded Cynthia for a moment before replying, "No, I don't believe you are. But I need to know what you know if I am to survive beyond 1891. No one knows who I am, where I am, or what I do. Because you know all three, I can't allow you to leave."

The two guards now loomed over Cynthia's head.

"Once you have breakfasted, you will be taken to your room until I have further need of you. I have had your strange apparatus moved here and I will be spending much of my day examining it. I have yet to decide your fate." To the guards, he said, "Don't let her leave. You know what will happen."

"No need to remind us, Professor."

Once locked inside, Cynthia pondered what to do.

What I wouldn't give for a few bars on my cell and a GPS satellite, she thought. *How did they communicate in this era? Carrier pigeons? Pony Express? Do they even have telephones?*

Feeling closed in, Cynthia went to one of the windows and drew the curtains aside. They appeared to be somewhere in the middle of London, part of what looked like a bunch of brick apartment houses on a narrow residential street. There was no front yard, just broad stone steps to the cobblestoned street. Carriages clip-clopped by, making Cynthia grateful to be on the second floor. Some children were playing jump ropes and some sort of ball game on the sidewalk nearby, showing that at least one thing hadn't changed. Cynthia found some comfort in that.

Only now did Cynthia realize what was truly different, what had been nagging at her once things had calmed down; no endless bombardment of electronic noise, no screens trying to sell her everything under the sun, no radios, no droning TV sets, no logos, no electronic beeping, no godawful music emanating from the carriages, no sirens, no billboards, no electronic clocks blasting the time whether you wanted to know it or not, and, best of all, no engine noise or petroleum fumes, Even the horse manure was preferable. Compared to Cynthia's era, all this seemed somewhat pastoral. Despite herself, she smiled.

And then came the answer.

Cynthia went to the bookshelf, where she saw, among other things, copies of *The Dynamics of an Asteroid* and *On the Nature of Time and Space*, both by Professor James Moriarty. She selected the larger of the two volumes and carefully removed a blank page from the front. She wrote a short note, folded the paper into a form no one in this century had ever seen, and prayed that certain things about armchairs had always been true.

Searching the cushions in the furniture, Cynthia found what she was looking for: a variety of coins, including two pieces of gold. She took a couple which looked like pennies and went back to the window. The games were still in progress as Cynthia threw the pennies to the kids, who looked up.

"Ma'am?" asked a young boy, age about eleven.

For all I know, this kid is an ancestor, she thought.

"Deliver something for me," Cynthia said as loud as she dared.

"What?"

With that, a paper airplane sailed from Cynthia's window gliding gently to the children below.

"Do you see the address?"

"Yes, ma'am."

The door burst open and one of the guards came in.

"Who're you talking to?" he demanded.

"I just want to know where I am," she said. "So I asked those kids."

"You'll be chained in the basement unless you know what's good for you," he growled. "Stay away from that window."

"All right."

Before stepping back, she spotted the boy who caught the paper airplane rounding the corner, already counting his coins.

CHAPTER THREE

The commotion began early in the evening, when Cynthia heard people shouting, running, and slamming doors. When the smoke started seeping under the crack in the door, she knew why.

"Hey!" she cried. "I'm locked in! Open this door!"

But her cries fell on deaf ears as she heard footsteps race by. She pounded her fists on the door. The smoke grew thicker. Cynthia ran to the window, opened it wide, and leaned out. A good twenty feet down onto a thick granite slab.

This is going to hurt, she thought, but found herself unable to move. *Maybe this is best for the future.*

The door burst open, and a man, squarely built and muscular, wearing a thick brown moustache and a black bowler hat, stepped in.

"Who—"

"Later! We don't have much time!"

"Wait!" Cynthia cried as she grabbed her purse. The man rolled his eyes, but he led Cynthia in the opposite direction everyone else was taking, toward the back of the house. They bolted down the rear stairway and out into the tiny backyard. The rear gate was open, and a growler waited in the alley, door open to receive them.

"Why are we waiting?"

"One more passenger to come."

No sooner had he said it than a tall, thin man wearing workman's clothing raced through the gate and dove through the growler's open door, with Cynthia's two guards in pursuit. Cynthia's rescuer tapped the roof a couple of times and the cab took off.

"I say, Holmes, that was close," said the man with the moustache, whom Cynthia found quite attractive. He had an athlete's body, but a doctor's face: kindness and understanding in his eyes, but leaving no doubt about the steel underneath.

"Who are you?" asked Cynthia.

"I thought you knew," said the tall man. "I am Sherlock Holmes, and this is my colleague, Doctor John Watson. You, we certainly hope, are Cynthia Kenyon. "

Cynthia nodded, her throat suddenly dry.

"Oh, my God," she said. "You're real!"

"Of course we are," Holmes replied. "I must congratulate you upon your ingenuity. How did you know to fold the paper in such a clever manner?"

"Back in school. We used to make paper airplanes all the time."

"Paper what?" Watson asked.

"So you know something of aerodynamics, too. You are an enigma, Miss Kenyon. We still don't know how you came to find us."

"It's a long story. Where are we going?"

"Home, of course," Holmes replied. "You knew our address. May I ask how? I am little known outside police and criminal circles."

"That's also a long story."

"Oh, where are my manners?" Watson said, handing over a hip flask. "You must be in need of fortification after your ordeal."

The brandy tasted harsh, but as the warm glow spread throughout Cynthia's system, she began to relax and get her bearings.

"Would you mind if we waited until we get to your apartment before I answer any questions?" she asked. "I have something to show you. Otherwise, you'll think I'm insane."

"I, too, would like better light," said Holmes. "Madam, from what I see, you cannot exist. Your scents are beyond my ken, other than their most unusual chemical composition. You show signs of having been vaccinated on more than one occasion, your purse is made of an artificial fabric unknown to me, and your shoes are in no style known anywhere on the Continent. All I can see for certain is that you're an American, lost, work in an office, and have a university education. Certainly, you don't know London very well. Yet you knew how to find us. The only logical conclusion is also an impossible one."

"Not necessarily." Cynthia raised the flask and asked, "May I?"

Watson nodded, and Cynthia took a second swallow. She handed the flask back to Watson, who handed it to Holmes. Watson took the last swallow.

As they clattered over the cobblestones, Cynthia became aware of warmth growing between herself and the doctor. She had always favored his physical type: squarely built and rugged, clearly an athlete, yet she found herself comforted by the kindliness in his manner and somewhat courtly attitude toward her. Cynthia had already seen the resolve that lay underneath. His moustache, of course, had always been a part of him and always would.

For his part, Watson clearly found Cynthia attractive; she had seen that look before on many a man, and it usually made her wary, but this was different. She felt something more, something which had been left out of her life for too long, that initial spark which always marks mutual attraction, and when their eyes met, both smiled.

Holmes muttered something that sounded disdainful, but refused to repeat it.

The cab pulled up in front of 221 Baker Street, where the three ascended the seventeen steps to Apartment B, solving one mystery.

Boy, can you tell men live here, she thought. Over near one of the windows, she saw an elaborate home laboratory and a portrait of someone who looked like one of her scowling ancestors

27

from Vermont over the fireplace, around which chairs and a sofa were arranged in a conversation circle. The heavy aroma of tobacco hung in the air, and half-full ashtrays occupied every table. One corner table had a small mountain of documents taking up most of the space. When Holmes lit a cigarette, Cynthia opened the window.

Watson placed a kettle on a large Bunsen burner, as Holmes settled into an armchair and gestured Cynthia to sit opposite him.

"Pray tell me of your predicament," Holmes said as Cynthia sat down.

"Before I do, I have to tell you I don't have any money."

"I do not do what I do for the money, Miss Kenyon. The work is its own reward, and your case promises many."

The kettle whistled.

"Do you have Earl Grey?" Cynthia asked.

"Yes," Watson replied, "it's my favorite. How do you know it?"

"Oh, I learned about it on *Next Generation* reruns. Captain Picard always—"

"I didn't understand a word of that," Holmes said. "What's a rerun? Who's Captain Picard?"

"He's the captain of the U.S.S. *Enterprise*."

"Do you come from a naval family?"

"Not really."

Cynthia retrieved her cell phone from her purse and activated it, amused by the responses to the opening ringtone. She handed it to Holmes.

"What is this?" he asked.

"It's called a cell phone," Cynthia said. "Where I come from, everyone has one of these. I can talk to almost anyone, anywhere. It has other functions, too, but I want you to see the photos."

"How is this possible?" Holmes asked. "Watson, take a look."

"Just press the little arrow on the right. Please bear with me."

Cynthia narrated the photos, as she had done with Moriarty.

"That's the Space Needle in Seattle. It hasn't been built yet. Here we are at the beach—" Cynthia noticed Watson's open approval of seeing her in a bikini, and blushed.

"I must say, there's no modesty left in America," he said. "The only half-naked women I ever see are in the examination room."

"Really? There was that memorable night—"

"Remember our guest, Holmes."

Well, I'd like to know more about that, Cynthia thought as she and Watson's eyes met and they shared a soft smile of amusement. Cynthia resumed her narrative.

"That's my sister, who drove down from Vermont last week, and here's my dad in that damn sports car—"

Cynthia stopped, her eyes starting to fill with tears.

"They haven't even been born yet and I'll never see them again," she said, restraining a sob.

Holmes handed the camera back as Watson handed her a handkerchief. Cynthia handed over her purse.

"Look at my driver's license and money," she said.

Holmes, his curiosity growing by the second, examined everything, his brow furrowed.

"You have devices far ahead of science, and your strange identification states that you won't be born for more than 100 years. Even your money looks different from American currency. If this is some sort of complex fraud, I cannot imagine what you hope to gain."

"What I hope to gain is your understanding that I have traveled backward in time! I have to get back to the damn machine which brought me here," she said. "Now you must think I'm insane."

"How did you end up at that house?" asked Holmes.

"I somehow ended up in the basement of a different house," she said. "I heard machinery, and I found two guys running some sort of metal stamping machine."

"Did you see electrical equipment?" Holmes asked.

"I wouldn't know what that looks like here. I asked their help in finding Professor Moriarty, and it turned out they worked for him."

"Professor Moriarty?" Watson asked. "Exactly who is that?"

Cynthia fell silent.

"You've never heard of him?"

They shook their heads. Holmes rose and pulled a thick scrapbook from his bookshelf.

"Moriarty, Professor James," he read. "Noted for his treatise on the binomial theorem, which won him the Mathematics Chair at St. Ursula's. His *Dynamics of an Asteroid* gained fame among both astronomers and mathematics, but reached such pinnacles of pure mathematics no one could properly evaluate it. His next work, *On the Nature of Time and Space*, however, was as widely reviled as his previous works praised, and he resigned his chair in disgrace. No mention of him after that."

"Let me ask you something," she said. "Purely hypothetical. Suppose you suddenly found yourself in the past. You know many things nobody else does about the future. What do you do?"

"What can you tell us about this period?" Holmes asked. "Our time."

"Not a lot," she admitted. "I didn't study much in the way of British history except for a couple of Shakespeare courses."

31

"Can you tell one thing that's going to happen in the near future?"

"Next year, toward the end of August, the volcano at Krakatoa will explode. It'll be one of the largest volcanic eruptions in history."

"I was hoping for a little nearer than that," said Holmes.

Cynthia slapped her head and said, "Doctor Watson, do you have a metal box with your name and the words, 'late Indian Army' on the lid?"

"Why, yes," he said. "How did you know that?"

Cynthia removed the envelope and tickets.

"My attorney found this on top of the things inside. "

"By Jove, Holmes! That's my handwriting!"

Cynthia sat back and smiled.

"When you have eliminated the impossible, whatever remains, however improbable, must be the truth," she said. She'd heard that in a *Star Trek* movie.

"I'll remember that," Holmes replied.

CHAPTER FOUR

Cynthia recapped her story for Holmes' and Watson's benefit, and showed them the photos of the time machine from the museum reception.

"Do you believe me now?"

"There is no other explanation for the present, but you will pardon me if I remain skeptical for the time being. Did you say this Moriarty had the machine on the premises where we found you?" Holmes asked.

Cynthia nodded.

"I have to tell you, Miss Kenyon, I searched the entire building and did not see anything like this device. "

"You never did tell me how you got me out."

"Simple enough. I dressed as a workman and said I was there about the plumbing. Every building in London can be counted on to need someone with those skills, so they let me inside, and I unstopped the drain causing problems. When I had a chance, I went into the kitchen and placed some smoke chemicals of my own devising inside the oven. After that, it was a matter of time."

"What do we do now, Mr. Holmes?" Cynthia asked. "I need that machine if I'm to have any hope of finding my friends and family again. For all I know, I've changed history already. I have no idea when you were supposed to learn of Professor

Moriarty, and now that he knows about you, your life could be in danger already."

"Perhaps you should prepare for bed, my dear," Watson said. "I happen to have some bedclothing I keep on hand for patients, and you may have my room. I'll sleep on the sofa."

"Oh, Doctor, I couldn't let you do that."

"I insist, and please call me John. We'll look at your situation in the morning. By then, Holmes will surely have a plan."

A sixtyish woman brought in supper for three, and plainly did not like what she saw in Apartment B.

"Mr. Holmes, I have been very liberal with you," she said, "your odd hours, more policemen than down the Old Bailey, and your rancid chemical experiments, but I cannot allow you to keep a woman in here. Think of my reputation!"

"Mrs. Hudson, you need not worry. Miss Kenyon is lost and has no money to return home. We, or at least I, am motivated purely by Christian charity. If anyone asks, she's my cousin from America, in town for a few days. You may rest assured she will leave here with her virtue intact."

Watson and Cynthia blushed. Feeling somewhat embarrassed, Cynthia looked down at the floor and tried not to show her grin. Eyeing Cynthia warily, Mrs. Hudson nodded and left. All burst out laughing.

"I can't say I'm not relieved about losing the corset," Cynthia said when the chuckles died down. "But she does have a point. People in this era get scandalized over things we ignore in my time."

"There is someone we must consult," Holmes said. "As it happens, you may be pleased to hear the name. Sir Christopher Kenyon, who heads the Royal Society of Theoretical Mathematics. You may also be interested to know that it is he who ruined Professor Moriarty's career at St. Ursula's."

"Founder of the Kenyon Scholarship?"

"You know it?"

"I heard about it the other day. That sounds strange, doesn't it? But he doesn't sound like a believer. He sounds like trouble."

"After he meets you, he'll almost certainly have to change his opinions. Which means he may be able to help refine Moriarty's theories into something practical."

"Mr. Holmes, we have to find the machine I came in. Can you imagine what might happen if Professor Moriarty learns how to use it?"

"One of many things we don't know is whether the machine can even move in two directions," Holmes said. "In any event, Sir Christopher is the Empire's best. Surely he can guide us."

"But what if he's a relative?" Cynthia asked. "We're heading into time paradox territory if we're not careful."

"Leave that to me."

The Royal Academy of Theoretical Mathematics was housed in a recently constructed three-story brick building which showcased the most garish aspects of Victorian architecture, from ornately chiseled stone facades right down to gargoyles with the faces of famous mathematicians from over the centuries.

"I really shouldn't be here," Cynthia said.

"Why not?" asked Holmes. "One does not simply walk into Sir Christopher's office when one feels like it. This appointment was difficult to secure on short notice."

"But I know things about advanced mathematics he doesn't," said Cynthia. "What if he discovers the special theory of relativity before Einstein?"

Damn, she thought, *I've said too much already.*

"Count yourself fortunate that your comment means nothing to either one of us," Holmes said. "Please don't say anything unless asked. This will be difficult enough."

Down the carpeted, oak-paneled hallway they went to the main office, and from there to Sir Christopher Kenyon's. Behind the door the three found a pleasant reception area, the walls lined with books and decorated with cheerful leafy plants, all sounds absorbed by a beautiful and intricately patterned Oriental carpet. A young man rose from behind a desk and introduced himself as Robert Wilson. He motioned for the visitors to sit down.

"Sir Christopher will be with you shortly. May I ask why this appointment is so urgently—I see."

"What?" Cynthia asked.

But she found out when Sir Christopher entered the room. Cynthia's heart almost skipped a beat.

That could be my dad! Cynthia thought. *He has to be an ancestor!*

"Please come in," the mathematician said, his tone frosty and distant. When the door closed, he got right to the point.

"Young lady, how did you find me?"

"What?"

"Your mother and I had an agreement, and I have honored it to the full. If this is some pathetic attempt at blackmail, you may be sure I'll get to Scotland Yard first. I won't—"

Sherlock Holmes burst out laughing.

"Sir Christopher, I assure you that before we came in here, we did not know of that particular situation," Holmes said. "We really are here on matters mathematical."

The eminent academic sank into the chair behind a desk that reminded Cynthia of an aircraft carrier.

"My apologies. It's just that this young lady could be my daughter. The resemblance is almost supernatural."

"Actually, you are closer to the mark than you think. This is Cynthia Kenyon, and we believe she is related to you. Miss Kenyon, may I see your device? I believe I can operate it now."

Cynthia handed the cell phone over, and Holmes punched some keys. He showed the screen to Kenyon.

"What is this?"

"One of your descendants from the 21st century."

"This is devilry!"

"Mr. Holmes, may I?"

Cynthia switched the phone over to its camera function, and snapped a photo of her ancestor. She also took the opportunity to take pictures of Holmes and Watson. After punching a few buttons, she handed the phone back and Sir Christopher was shocked to see his own face looking back from the tiny screen.

"What are you telling me?"

"That Professor James Moriarty was right."

"That mountebank? Nonsense."

"Sir Christopher, she has persuaded me," Holmes said, "and there is no higher court of appeal in the establishment of fact. This woman is your descendant, and she has come to you to ask your help in returning to where she belongs."

Sir Christopher pulled a cord hanging behind him and young Wilson entered the room.

"Wilson, will you please prepare tea for our guests and bring in a copy of the Moriarty monstrosity, as well? Thank you."

"What was it about Moriarty's theory upset you, Sir Christopher?"

"To be honest, I prefer 'Professor.' Anyway, to spare you the agony of his prose, I'll put it like this. Moriarty does not believe that events move through time in a smooth flow, as the hours do ticking off on a clock. He sees time as more of a river, with currents, pools, and suchlike. He believes that the reason it takes a watched pot longer to boil is that time actually does slow down. He has used his theories to explain ghosts and suchlike, calling their appearance 'time slips.' One does not see a ghost; one sees the living person through a ripple in the time stream. Complete twaddle, and an embarrassment to the Royal Society. You can see how I couldn't allow him to continue."

"To continue your original metaphor, thanks to the device which brought Miss Kenyon here, we can now navigate that river. Miss Kenyon, will you please show him?"

Cynthia showed the photo to the professor.

"You came in that?"

Cynthia nodded.

"That disk in the back is a solar collector," she said. "How it works on the inside, I just don't know."

"You mean to say it runs on sunlight?"

"Converted to electricity, yes."

"There is another wrinkle, Professor Kenyon. Moriarty has the machine. He could be anywhere in time, doing anything."

"If you'll forgive me, this is ... overwhelming. Could we meet some other time, when I've had a chance to read the treatise again and consider its implications?"

"Gladly. Shall we come by, say, in two days?"

"That should give me enough time. Make an appointment with Wilson."

"Oh, yes, one other thing, Sir Christopher. Please keep this to yourself as much as possible."

"Who would believe me?"

Once outside, Holmes said, "I have an errand of pressing urgency, Miss Kenyon, and so I commend you to the good doctor's care. The Criterion at seven? Splendid."

Watson's face expressed both relief and anticipation.

"Alone at last," said Watson, with a smile in his eyes.

"So what does a girl from twenty-first century America do all day in nineteenth century London?"

"I should say that someone with your sense of adventure would certainly enjoy a day at the races. Fancy the ponies, by any chance?"

"My grandmother would take us to Saratoga every year."

"So some things in America do last. Excellent. We're off to Alexandra Park."

The Alexandra Park raceway was part of the vast grounds of North London's Alexandra Palace, which ruled the skyline with magnificent splendor. The course itself was unlike anything Cynthia had ever seen before. More of a pear shape than an oval, it had an extra lane that stretched away from the main course.

"That's for the five furlong races," Watson explained. "They're running a shorter course this afternoon."

Cynthia found it comforting to be away from the city for a while, especially the soot that seemed to cover everything left outside for too long. Over the next few hours, she found herself becoming closer to Watson, taking comfort in his strength, his confidence, his masculinity. During one race, her fingers intertwined with his as if it were the most natural thing in the world, and when he put his arm around her waist, it felt so comfortable, so right.

I've never met anyone like him, she thought. *We just don't have men like this anymore.*

"My turn to bet," she said, taking a racing form. "Please put a pound for me on that one."

"Slow and Steady? At twenty to one?"

"Slow and steady wins the race," Cynthia said simply, and the doctor made his way toward the betting window to, no doubt, throw his money away. She could have sworn she heard him say, "Women!" under his breath.

Maybe I'm looking at this all wrong, she thought, struck again by the lack of advertising anywhere, and the only noise in the crowd coming from human beings and animals, nothing artificial. *They don't have nuclear reactor meltdowns here, no school shootings, no infomercials, no talk radio, no fast food. All I have to do is stay out of history's way.*

Then she remembered the note from Leo's grandmother: "History depends on it."

"The flag's been waved," Watson said. "Here they come!"

The horses seemed to be evenly matched, with the favorite, Hooves Galore, out in front, but Slow and Steady moved up from the middle, and on the outside. The cluster began to thin as some of the horses fell back, but Slow and Steady kept on, closing in on Hooves Galore.

Closer.

Closer still.

"She's ahead!" Cynthia cried. "Look, John! She's going to—"

The air filled with groans, a few cheers, and torn tickets as Slow and Steady clocked in a half a length ahead of Hooves Galore.

"Slow and Steady wins the race," Watson said, and before Cynthia knew it, she was receiving a warm and powerful kiss. Its fire spread through her body much like the brandy did, and when it broke, she found herself a little dizzy.

"Wow," she said.

"I've been wanting to do that since we met," Watson said. "Well, we have some real money for the rest of the day. How would you like to spend it?"

"On clothes," she said. "I've got to get out of this dress."

The doctor smiled, filling Cynthia with a warm feeling of desire. Now she initiated the kiss, and it felt more intimate.

"Great minds think alike," she said.

They registered at a small downtown hotel as Mr. and Mrs. John Watson, and once alone, they let their passions loose, kissing, coupling, chatting, and kissing once more. Cynthia didn't want that afternoon ever to end.

Cynthia rolled to face Watson during one of their breaks.

"Cynthia, must you go back? Couldn't you stay with me?"

"What about Holmes?"

"Hang Holmes. He'll be able to manage without me. It's not as if we're married. Remind me to send a telegram canceling our dinner date."

Cynthia moved closer and placed her head on Watson's shoulder, reveling in the feel of his warm naked flesh against hers.

"I don't know what my staying would do to history," she said.

"I simply want what every decent man wants," he said. "A wife. A family. A son to carry my name. I'm alone in the world. If I don't have children, the Watson name dies with me."

"You're not proposing, are you?"

"No, of course not. Please don't think me impetuous or selfish. But I'm going to be thirty next month. Other men my age have established themselves in their profession. I'm still adrift."

"Maybe Professor Moriarty has crashed the damn thing in a desert in Mongolia and the Huns got him," Cynthia said. "Then I'd have no choice."

Watson laughed, and kissed Cynthia again.

CHAPTER FIVE

Cynthia and Watson spent the next morning with another bout of lovemaking, and, after a breakfast of ham, eggs, toast and coffee, they found some new clothes for Cynthia.

"Do they have pockets in any of these dresses?" she asked. "I really need my cell phone with me. It's the only way to prove anything."

"I'll arrange for it," Watson promised.

When Cynthia and Watson returned to Baker Street the next day, they found Sherlock Holmes at his laboratory table, examining a coin under his magnifying glass.

"Watson, take a look at this," he said without looking up. "It's extraordinary. Please sit down, Miss Kenyon."

Watson joined Holmes, who asked him, "What do you see?"

"A gold sovereign."

"No, you're looking at a brilliant copy. See what happens when I scrape it."

Holmes took a scalpel and scratched at the metal. Underneath the gold he found grayish metal.

"I think it's an alloy of some sort, with gold plating through electrolysis. But the engineering is remarkable, don't you agree?"

"Where did you get it?"

"I have new clients: some officials from Her Majesty's Treasury came in this morning. These are cropping up all over London, and I believe Miss Kenyon can help us track—oh, no."

"Mr. Holmes?"

"You two are falling in love, aren't you?"

"Does it show that much?" Cynthia asked.

"I am Sherlock Holmes. Of course it shows. Watson, how could you lead the poor girl on in such a manner? She must return to her own time."

"But what if she prefers to remain?" asked Watson. "What if that is her destiny?"

"Miss Kenyon has said it herself: she may have already altered history by bringing Professor Moriarty into my life too soon. Who knows what other chains of events she may have set in motion?"

Cynthia remembered a line from a movie, and repeated it: "The future is not yet set. There is no fate but what we make."

"Miss Kenyon, you were most eager to return to the future. I agree. Your liaison with Doctor Watson has clouded your judgment."

"Mr. Holmes, despite all you've done for me, it's still my life. Besides, apparently I have a sibling of sorts here, somewhere. I need time to think and decide what I want. In any event, the future hasn't happened yet. What if my coming here stops a war, or results in some sort of scientific breakthrough? Maybe I'm here for good reasons."

Holmes surrendered, dropped into his armchair and lit a pipe. Watson led Cynthia from the room.

"I can't deny what I want," he said, taking Cynthia in his arms. "My heart yearns for fulfillment. If you were to remain and become my wife one day, I believe we could be quite happy."

"I know, John," she said. "This changes everything. Besides," she added with a ribald smile, "you're a tiger."

Watson's smile twinkled. They shared a kiss.

"I must go to Bart's," he said. "I have some patients there. I'll return this afternoon." Watson kissed Cynthia's hand and said, "'Til then."

When she returned to the sitting room, Holmes had finished his pipe, but still pondered.

"Miss Kenyon, have you an idea of how long it will take before you decide what you want to do?"

"I know, I know, I'm breaking up the boys' club. You look like the rest of the Beatles must have felt when Yoko Ono came onto the scene."

"What?"

"Beyond your time, Mr. Holmes. My apologies. You see, the world is completely different in my time. I wish I knew what was safe to tell you."

"As do I. It's a pity you're a woman. A man with your knowledge could—"

"We're past that sexist garbage in my time," Cynthia snapped. "I have an education, a job, and I live on my own. Women are equal to men in twenty-first century America. It won't be too long before a woman is President of the United States."

"So that hasn't happened yet, even in the far future? Interesting. Whatever you decide, Moriarty and that time machine must be found. Who knows what power it could give him? Besides, we certainly can't return you to the future without it."

"What about the counterfeit coin? Where does that fit in?"

"You told me that when you found yourself here, two men were operating a metal stamping press. I believe they were making these. That house will lead us to the professor, if I am not mistaken, and from there, of course, to the machine."

"But I don't know where the house is."

"If I may."

Holmes held his magnifying glass over Cynthia's hands, examining them minutely, paying particular attention to Cynthia's long nails.

"Let us be grateful for vanity," he said. "You were held in a house in north London, not far from Marylebone, if my poor powers of deduction serve me."

"How can you possibly know that?"

"From the grit under your nails. It's all from the same area, and of course you know about Alexandra Park, where Watson's rent money often winds up. You haven't been able to wash as thoroughly as you'd like, so plenty of grit remains if you look closely enough."

"How will that help you find the house?"

"By itself, not. But if we could find Wiggins, we could—"

"Wiggins?"

"The ragamuffin you sent here the other day. Young boys are invaluable as spies. We know the neighborhood. Come."

Two hours later, Cynthia, Sherlock Holmes, and young Wiggins stood before an anonymous wooden house with a scrawny front yard.

"How will I know?" she asked.

"Take a peek in the front window and tell me if you recognize the parlor."

Cynthia found a gap in the curtain and looked in. It was all there: the tables covered with lace, gas lamps, books, still no TV.

It's so strange to look at a living room with no TV, she thought. *I'll never get used to that.*

"That's it," she said.

Holmes handed Wiggins a shilling.

"There's more where that came from," he said. "Wait outside, but don't be seen. I shall have instructions soon."

"Yes, sir!" the boy replied.

"How do we get in?"

"I've always found the front door convenient."

Holmes reached into his frock coat's pocket and produced a skeleton key, which he used to open the door. They ducked inside.

At first, all seemed quiet, but then Cynthia heard the familiar sound of the metal press, stamping out sheets of fake sovereigns.

"That's it."

"Very good. Here's cab fare. Get to Scotland Yard and find Inspector Lestrade. Make sure he brings a spare bobby or two. Tell Wiggins to stand watch, but remain out of sight. Don't tarry."

Cynthia raced into the street and found Wiggins, then a cab.

Scotland Yard proved to be a stone and brick building about six stories tall, and bustling with policemen, attorneys, administrators and criminals. Not knowing what else to do, Cynthia accosted the first constable she saw and asked, "Where can I find Inspector Lestrade?"

"Inside, miss. His office is on the second floor."

Scotland Yard reminded Cynthia of the ancient, dilapidated building in which she spent her elementary school years: drab walls, tight corridors, terrible ventilation, and tiny, cramped offices. She stopped at the nameplate "Insp. G. Lestrade," and knocked.

"Come!"

Behind a small scarred cherrywood desk sat a short man, about Cynthia's height, his thin hair swept back, his narrow face and sharp nose and chin reminding Cynthia somewhat of a ferret.

"Yes, miss? What can I do for you?"

"Sherlock Holmes sent me to find you. He's located a counterfeit coin operation at this address. He said you should bring backup."

"Bring what?"

"Cops, bring a couple of extra cops."

"Right you are."

"I have a cab waiting."

"He's trained you well, has our Mr. Holmes."

Lestrade stuck his head into the corridor.

"Rance! Monroe! Snap to!"

"Yes, sir!" they replied.

CHAPTER SIX

The cab arrived at the counterfeiting house, but the open front door told Cynthia everything she needed to know.

"Best wait here, miss," Lestrade told her. "No place for a woman."

"Look in the basement first. You'll find the press there."

"Rance, stay out front and don't let anybody in. Monroe, follow me."

Lestrade and the stout Monroe walked inside. Cynthia heard their voices, but knew something had happened to Holmes, something which possibly made up her mind for her.

What have I done? she thought as her stomach suddenly clenched. *What if I've gotten the greatest detective in history killed?*

Lestrade returned in about fifteen minutes.

"If I may, Miss Kenyon, I'd like to send Rance to Her Majesty's Treasury to let them know what we've found. I daresay you may have reward coming for this."

"What about Holmes?"

"There's no one in there. We found overturned furniture and obvious signs of a fight."

"Oh, God!"

"There, there, we'll find him. Don't ever tell him this, but we've rather come to depend on him at the Yard. No one wants to lose him."

"I have an idea," Cynthia said. "Master Wiggins? Where are you?" she called.

The boy emerged from his hiding spot.

"Please tell Inspector Lestrade what happened."

"I don't know," the boy said. "I heard some harsh words through the window, and sounds of people fighting, furniture breaking, and the like. Two rough-looking types came up in a growler and I saw them force Mr. Holmes into it."

"How long ago?"

"Don't know."

"You remember the house where you found me?"

"Yes, ma'am."

"Take us there."

"Not just yet."

Lestrade gave Wiggins a shilling and some instructions, as Monroe stood by the front door of the building.

"The boy is getting some more help," Lestrade said as he took a seat opposite Cynthia. "We'll deliver Mr. Holmes safe and sound, don't you worry about that."

One of the wooden wheels hit a loose rock, and Cynthia almost fell. Instinctively, she felt around for a seat belt, but of course there was none.

I had no idea transportation was so painful, thought Cynthia as the cab bounced along the streets at what seemed to Cynthia's modern sense of speed to be ridiculously slow and bouncing was so bad it sometimes jarred Cynthia's teeth.

"Don't you people have shock absorbers?" she snapped.

"I'm sorry if our facilities don't match your lofty standards, Miss Kenyon," the inspector said. "We'll be there soon enough."

Are we even going ten miles an hour? Cynthia wondered.

When they arrived, several other officers were waiting at the corner. Lestrade sent two of them somewhere, and stationed one in front of the house and the other two flanked him as he knocked on the door with some vigor.

"Police! Open up!" he demanded.

Cynthia heard a *click!* as someone locked the door.

"Right," Lestrade said. "On my mark."

The three men smashed their shoulders against the thick, heavy door a few times, but it gave way and slammed open, spilling Lestrade and one of his officers onto the floor while the other ran inside, shouting, "Police!"

All Cynthia heard was a commotion inside, while the remaining officer joined in. Men shouting, sounds of a fight, furniture and glass smashing. Unable to wait, she went inside herself and saw Lestrade struggling with Harry, one of the counterfeiters. Picking up a vase, she threw it at him, getting him squarely on the crown. He cried out even as the vase continued and bounced off Lestrade. Cynthia jumped on Harry's back, and that took him to the floor. Lestrade had the handcuffs out, and Harry's hands were quickly locked together behind his back.

"Thanks, but next time leave the policing to me, eh?" Lestrade said, hauling Harry to his feet and tossing him on the sofa. He handed Cynthia a nightstick.

"If he makes a move, give him a good one in the noggin and don't be a lady about it," Lestrade said. "Where's Sherlock Holmes, boyo?"

"Downstairs," Harry replied, trying to catch his breath.

"Somebody get in here!" yelled Lestrade. "We need a wagon right quick!"

A new bobby came in from somewhere and took Cynthia by the arm.

"Best get you someplace safe," he said. "No place for a woman here. This is man's work. Give me the nightstick."

Cynthia handed it over and the bobby led her outside and hailed the cab. He joined her inside and gave the cabby an address in south London.

"Really, I don't need an escort," she said. "Inspector Lestrade is being too protective."

"But Professor Moriarty is expecting you," the cop said, and displayed a derringer. "If you know what's best, you'll just sit there quietly and follow instructions, eh?"

With that, he put the tiny pistol away and placed the nightstick on his lap.

Cynthia wanted to cry, but would not give her captor the satisfaction.

"Where are we going?" she asked.

"You'll find out soon enough."

Three knocks from the cabbie.

"What is it?" asked Cynthia's captor.

"Looks like we're being followed, sir."

The man swore and looked out the back in time to see another cab drop back. He handed his own cabbie a five-pound note and said, "Lose them."

"Sir!"

That proved not to be an easy promise to keep, because the pursuing cab kept anticipating their moves, but suddenly Cynthia's cab went down a narrow alley at full gallop, and they came out in a dirty side street.

"Well done, driver!" the false officer called.

After a few more unexpected detours to make sure, the cab stopped at a wharf on the Thames, where a steamboat waited. Cynthia's captor led her to it and made her get on board, where she was taken to a cramped and tiny cabin by two silent, mean and grubby sailors. They locked her in.

As the boat chugged toward the sea, Cynthia could have sworn she heard John Watson's voice crying, "Holmes! They have her!"

The thought that she might never see Watson again pained her to the core, and for the first time, she allowed herself tears.

CHAPTER SEVEN

After docking, Cynthia was blindfolded and placed in a horse-drawn carriage. All she knew was that night had fallen. No one around her spoke, and the events of the day caught up with her. She fell asleep.

The blindfold came off when the carriage stopped. The darkness around them seemed total, and the air cool, fresh and sweet; they were no longer in the city, and the clean country air invigorated her. A man lit a lamp and said, "Take her inside."

Soon the outline of a chateau became visible in the darkness; light glowed through the windows in at least three floors. The men led Cynthia up wide stone steps to the front door, where she was taken to an ornate sitting room.

This could be a museum, Cynthia thought as she took in the tapestries depicting country life and medieval battles, the finely crafted furniture, paintings of pastoral countrysides and portraits of notables from previous centuries on the smooth, emerald green walls. An elaborate tea service, warm to the touch, sat on a sideboard, and Cynthia poured a cup to ease her parched throat. At that moment, the tall doors opened and the lean, reptilian figure of Professor James Moriarty entered.

"My dear, you have seriously inconvenienced me," he said. "You have cost me a great deal of money and forced me into hiding on the Continent. I require restitution."

"Professor, you can't blame me for outsmarting you."

"If you value your safety, Miss Kenyon, you will answer every question fully and honestly, and do exactly as you are told. You will also display courtesy at all times."

"All right."

"Who is Sherlock Holmes? Who is his partner?"

"You don't know?"

Moriarty slapped her.

"Enough! Do I need stronger measures?"

Cynthia shook her head and sat down.

"Who is Sherlock Holmes?"

"He's a private detective. Scotland Yard uses him to solve troublesome cases."

"And his fame apparently lasts into the 21st century."

"He's considered to be the greatest detective who ever lived, and you are his most famous enemy."

"How did you know to contact him?"

"I found it in the city directory in the room where you locked me," Cynthia lied. "It's not as if I have anyone else to turn to."

"If you hadn't escaped, you might have lived the life of a queen," Moriarty said. "With your machine, we could have plundered the centuries without fear and retired to lives of luxury. But you are headstrong, Miss Kenyon, and I can't have that."

The penny dropped.

"You can't figure it out, can you?" Cynthia said. "You can't make the machine work!"

"It has proven a frustration. You will help me understand some of that odd circuitry which apparently holds the key."

"Professor Moriarty, I'm an editor, not an engineer."

"You have some familiarity and you are the only one who has used the device. Tomorrow morning, we go to work. Estelle will lead you to your room and draw you a bath if you wish it."

"Thank you, Professor."

A serving maid appeared in the doorway, and Cynthia followed her without complaint. She knew she was under surveillance. Estelle led Cynthia up a wide, elaborate, thickly carpeted staircase to a room on the third floor, where a hot bath was already waiting.

"Are we alone?" Cynthia asked, whispering.

"We are, miss," the young woman whispered in reply.

"But you are instructed to report to the professor anything I might say."

Estelle, nervous, nodded.

"Are you a prisoner here?"

Again, Estelle nodded.

"If I help you, will you help me?"

Now Estelle looked over her shoulder and whispered, "You don't know what it's like here. You don't want to be a woman in the professor's employ."

"We'll talk tomorrow."

Aloud, Estelle said, "Very good, Miss. I apologize, but I must lock you in."

"I understand. Good night, Estelle."

A chance for real cleanliness at last! Cynthia took full advantage of it, scouring every inch of her skin. Somewhat dismayed that shampoo hadn't been invented yet, at least they made soap intended for hair care, and she cleaned her hair as thoroughly as possible.

They really need to learn about personal hygiene, she thought. *Maybe I'm here to invent shampoo and then John and I can retire as rich industrialists.*

Once clean and in fresh bedclothes, Cynthia pulled her cell phone out from its hiding place in her skirt, using it to take a picture of the well-appointed room she was in, particularly the canopied bed.

What I wouldn't give for a few bars out here, she thought, and then remembered: she had taken a picture of the time machine's dashboard.

This was the first time Cynthia had a chance to take a really good look at it. She didn't see the complete dashboard, but it was clear that modern engineers decided to have a little fun, using LCD displays to show the intended date of arrival, a keypad, and a computer display. If she could scope out the password … or did she simply need to reset it and put the lever back in place? And what about the power? Was there even any left?

Deactivating the cell phone (how much more battery power did it have left, anyway?), Cynthia hid it under her pillow and fell asleep.

CHAPTER EIGHT

No one trusted Cynthia when she was taken to the Moriarty's laboratory. Two guards armed with nightsticks never allowed more than two feet of distance between them, trained dogs roamed the halls as well as the grounds, and the guards locked every door after they passed through.

I've got to find John! Cynthia thought.

"Good morning, Miss Kenyon. I hope you had a good night's sleep. We have a long day ahead of us. I want you to show me everything you know about this machine."

"Most of what I know won't be any help," she said. "If I could get inside, I might—"

"Don't insult my intelligence!" the professor snapped. "I will point to a device and you will tell me what it does." He said something in French, and one of the guards stepped next to her.

"If you make a sudden move, Raoul will strike you, and I can promise you it will hurt. Now tell me what the devices do and their specific function."

The professor gestured and a young man with a notebook stepped over.

"Donald will be transcribing our conversation," Moriarty said, and it occurred to Cynthia that might be a good idea.

"Before we begin, Professor, might I visit the privy?"

At least I'm learning the lingo, Cynthia thought.

"Yes, of course," Moriarty said. "Thank you for thinking of it before we begin. Such distractions get in the way of progress. But Raoul will be listening."

Cynthia was amazed to find a flush toilet and a wash basin, the first she'd seen since her arrival. But what really mattered was the open window which ventilated the small room. Standing on the seat, she peered out to see a high and thick stone wall, but beyond it lay bright sunshine and a pastoral countryside, rolling green hills, and sheep, with small farms dotting the landscape.

After flushing the toilet, Cynthia got her cell phone out and activated the voice recorder, even though she risked draining the remaining power.

Over the course of the morning, Cynthia explained the machine as well as she could, identifying the onboard computer, the display, and the computer, which caught the professor's particular interest.

"Does it calculate numbers?" he asked.

"It's capable of making millions of calculations per second," replied Cynthia. "It's quite powerful."

"How do I activate it?"

"Start with the red button."

The Acoreous Museum's logo appeared on the screen, with a little electronic classical music. Then the cursor blinked next to the password bar.

"Password? What is it?"

"I don't know," Cynthia said. "It took off when I accidentally hit that—"

It was already on! she realized. *Maybe I'm not alone here!*

"Anyway, a password is usually a mix of letters, numbers and special characters. They're very difficult to guess. But I have an idea."

"Tell me."

"It's probably better if I do it," said Cynthia. "You've never used one before."

"No tricks, Miss Kenyon. You will learn, and learn quickly, that I don't have a forgiving nature."

Cynthia got onto the seat, large enough for two. Moriarty climbed in after her. Cynthia typed the word "Acoreous," which was rejected.

"Try something else," Moriarty said, irritated.

Cynthia tried everything she could think of: name and number combinations, some of her own passwords, random key strikes. Nothing.

"I'm sorry, Professor, it's no good. Perhaps you've got the mind for it, but I don't."

"Very well."

Cynthia explained the GPS screen, now useless with satellites as least 80 years in the future.

"This one's important," she said. "It shows how much power we have left."

The trip had taken a considerable bite of the power supply: about one-third.

"Unless you can find a lot of megawattage, Professor, I don't think you'll be going too far," Cynthia said.

"If it exists, it can be found," Moriarty said.

They continued for several more hours: Moriarty's supply of questions proved inexhaustible. Cynthia realized she couldn't tell him everything; it was becoming clear her chances of staying alive diminished the less useful she became to the Professor.

"You have done well today, Miss Kenyon," he said at last. "Few women could have maintained such calm in these circumstances. You could be most useful in my organization. Please consider it."

"It's an honor to be asked, Professor Moriarty, truly."

For the first time, something resembling a smile from the ordinarily stern mathematician.

"I have a great deal of information to consider," he said. "The guards will return you to the chateau. We dine at seven."

Once alone, Cynthia checked the cell phone's battery: low power, in need of recharging.

Great, now I can't use it again for 150 years, she thought.

CHAPTER NINE

A uniformed guard shook Cynthia's shoulder and said something in French. He appeared angry. Conscious of being clad only in a nightgown, Cynthia pulled the blanket up over her body.

"What is this?" she demanded.

"American," the guard said, his voice heavy with a French accent. "I might have known. Have you been here all night?"

"Of course, I was locked in here."

"That is not possible."

As Cynthia's head cleared, she saw that the room was cordoned off with velvet ropes, with tourists peering through the door, trying to get a good view. Some of them were taking pictures with their cell phones. It gave her a strange feeling of disorientation.

"Please find me something to wear," she said. "Where am I?"

"You are in the Chateau Duquesne," the guard said. "We are about 25 kilometers southwest of Paris. How do you come to be here?"

"I—don't know."

"Do you need a doctor?"

Cynthia reached under her pillow, relieved to find her cell phone had also made the trip.

"I don't think so," she said. "I'm completely lost. Are there any Americans here?"

"Please come with me."

Feeling vulnerable in the nightgown, Cynthia did not protest as the guard led her down the hall. Everything had changed. The 21st century suddenly bombarded Cynthia with its cacophony of electronics, bustle, and urgency. Where last night she was a prisoner in the most elegant of country cages, today she was a vagabond with nothing but a cell phone, a nightgown and an insane story. What had been comfortable furniture only a few hours (now many years) ago was off limits, tourists wandered about, staring and taking pictures as Cynthia was led past them. Air conditioning, electric light, music over loudspeakers (how intrusive it seemed now) … she had come back to her present, but how close?

"What day is it?" she asked.

"It is September 14," the guard replied.

Thanks a lot, Cynthia thought, knowing what the guard would think if she asked the year.

One of the costumed docents found Cynthia some period clothing, and once again Cynthia was dressed like someone from the 19th century. The guard led Cynthia to an office that had been the study down the hall from her room. It didn't look much different: walls of books, portraits of the chateau's previous denizens, photographs of landscapes, a sofa, coffee table with magazines, a steaming coffee pot by the desk on which, thank

God, she saw a flatscreen computer. The guard bade her to sit down, as an attractive man a few years older than she came into the room, and spoke to the guard in French.

When the guard left, the man said, "I'm Guy Harrison. I'm the historical director here. May I ask who you are?"

"You're not French."

"No, I'm on sabbatical from the University of Massachusetts. May I have your name, please?"

"My name? Cynthia Kenyon."

Harrison registered a look of shock.

"You've been missing for months," he said. "You vanished from a museum in front of a dozen witnesses. Where have you been?"

"You'll have me put away if I tell you."

"I'm all ears."

Cynthia hesitated, thinking, *No matter what I say, he'll think I'm crazy.*

Cynthia bit her lip for a moment and finally said, "I've been in 1882."

Harrison poured two cups of coffee from the pot, reminding Cynthia she was ravenously hungry.

"Ms. Kenyon, if that's true, you may hold the key to a longstanding mystery," he said, picking up his phone and saying something in French. "Now, please tell me what happened."

Cynthia told him most of the story – how she came to be in the time machine, her adventures in London (omitting the tryst with Watson), and ending with her encounter with Moriarty at the chateau.

"Professor Moriarty? Who's that?" Harrison seemed amazed. "And who is Sherlock Holmes?"

"You've never heard of Sherlock Holmes? He's the most famous detective in history!"

"Not in France, I'm afraid."

"No, I can prove it."

Taking out her cell phone, she went to the pictures menu and found the photos she had taken of Moriarty and Holmes when they first met. Harrison glanced at it without comment.

He thinks I'm a lunatic, she thought.

"There is no record of his being here. As far as I've been able to tell, no one lived here during the late 19th century."

Cynthia shook her head.

"The professor is a master of covering his tracks," she said.

She showed Harrison other pictures, including Sherlock Holmes, Watson, and her ancestor, Sir Christopher Kenyon.

"I don't know any of them," Harrison said.

"Funny hat? Magnifying glass? Cape?"

"Means nothing to me. I can see from the photo that Sir Christopher must be a relative."

"You know something?" Cynthia said. "There's an entire branch of the family nobody knows about. Sir Christopher told me he had a daughter out of wedlock, and thought I was she when I showed up at his office. He looks just like my father. My God, I should call them, shouldn't I?"

That's when the cell phone battery ran out. Cynthia cursed.

"What was it you said about Moriarty's theories concerning the nature of time?"

"Professor Moriarty believed that time doesn't flow in a straight line from one moment to the next. He believed time was more like a river, with currents, tributaries, and the like. He believed there was a way to navigate the river. He said that ripples in the time pool were responsible when people saw ghosts, for instance. It's not that they're spirits, it's more like the same moment in time is recurring in the current. He called them 'time slips.'"

Harrison stared at her for a moment and then said, "Oh, my God. The Versailles time slip."

"The what?"

"The Palace of Versailles is not far from here," Harrison said. "Very early in the 20th century, two women were touring the grounds, and they came across people in period costume. The trees looked different, and they spotted a man who might have been a French noble. One of the women believed they had actually greeted Marie Antionette. Scholars at the time laughed, of course, because they described things which weren't there in the 20th century. But years later, archeologists found evidence of a bridge the two had crossed, and discovered some aspects of the buildings they could not have known about. They believed they had traveled back in time temporarily."

"And they just walked back into their own time?"

"That's it. They were only in the past for about half an hour or so."

"So Professor Moriarty was right. That explains what happened to me."

"Let me make a phone call."

The door opened, and a woman brought in a tray with French pastries and fruit.

"Thank God," she said. "I'm famished. Is there something we can do about clothes? I can't wear these all day."

"Professor Hartke, please," Harrison said. "Astrophysics … right. Tell him it's about Versailles. … Paul, it's Guy Harrison. I've got a live one for you. I'm putting Cynthia Kenyon on the phone. She claims to have had a time slip."

Cynthia heard the startled "What?" even from her seat. She put her coffee down and took the phone.

"Professor Hartke?"

"Yes, that's right. What makes you think you've experienced a time slip?"

"Let me ask you something first. Have you ever heard of Professor James Moriarty?"

"Yes, I've studied his work as part of my research into the Versailles time slip. Are you a math student?"

"Moriarty was right," Cynthia said. "If you know the Acoreus Museum, then you know one of their people built a time machine based on Moriarty's theories and plans drawn up by H.G. Wells. I wound up in it by accident and landed in 1882. But now I've come back to the present without it. How is that possible?"

"Let's use Moriarty's river metaphor to keep things simple. If you view time as a river, then it has different currents, tributaries and the like. Since Guy's the one calling me, I'm going to assume you found a pool near the riverbank, as it were."

"Why me?"

"Perhaps because, having traveled in time before, it's easier for you to find the time stream. We will need to talk, Ms. Kenyon. Could we meet sometime?"

"I need to make arrangements to get home. Could we talk after that?"

"Take my number."

"Better give me your sizes," Harrison said. "I'll pick a few things up from a department store. Feel free to use my computer and my cell phone. I won't be gone long."

"Thank you, Professor."

Cynthia spent the next hour calling people and reassuring them she was all right, but avoiding a real explanation of what had happened, figuring it would be better when she had her cell phone back with real evidence. Her parents made plans to come to

71

France immediately to pick her up, and then Cynthia checked her social media accounts.

The posts gave Cynthia a feeling of attending her own funeral. She found eulogies, apologies, notes from old boyfriends, and links to Web sites about the disappearance, which had gone viral because of the time machine.

These Web sites are insane, Cynthia thought. *Is there anything people won't believe?* She called her mother back and got the voice mail.

"Mom, it's Cynthia. Don't tell anybody I'm back just yet, okay? I'm looking at all these Web sites that have me kidnapped by aliens, showing up in old photographs, and on one of them I'm supposed to have been Charlotte Corday. We're going to be bombarded when I turn up. You and Dad just keep it to yourselves, please?"

That led to something else. How could an historian, of all people, never have heard of Sherlock Holmes? Cynthia found a search engine and ran a check. Contrary to her expectations, there was very little to be found: no photographs of Jonny Lee Miller, Benedict Cumberbatch, Jeremy Brett or Basil Rathbone, none of Watson's accounts, nothing. Eventually she found a Web site dedicated to the history of forensic science. The illustration looked nothing like Holmes.

"**SHERLOCK HOLMES (1854-1924?)** Sherlock Holmes is considered to be one of the founders of police science. He is credited with calculating a suspect's height from the length of his stride, and the first to preserve footprints and tracks in plaster of Paris for comparison purposes. Holmes was also a scholar, whose interests ranged from early music to biology. His death remains a mystery. It is believed he drowned while swimming and his body washed out to sea, but it was never found."

What happened? Cynthia wondered as she entered the name of "John H. Watson, M.D." All that produced were references to contemporary physicians, so she had to dig a little deeper, adding "London 1882." That produced entirely different results, all on Web sites devoted to Queen Victoria. One read:

"The last attempt on the Queen was thwarted by the sacrifice of one of her subjects on the occasion of the Queen's Golden Jubilee in 1887. The Queen was entering Windsor Station for her return to Buckingham Palace. Dr. John H. Watson was among those hoping to get a glimpse of their monarch when someone fired a rifle. The Queen would have been hit, but Watson spotted the rifle and threw himself in front of the Queen just in time. As he bled to death, he last words were, 'I have served my Queen and I die a happy man.' Jubilee celebrations were subsequently canceled for the day, and the Queen attended Watson's funeral the following week."

No! Cynthia thought. *That didn't happen! I have to go back!*

"There's never a TARDIS around when you need one," Guy Harrison said when he returned and heard what Cynthia had discovered.

"You've got to let me back into that room," Cynthia said. "I can't let him die like that!"

"Cynthia, Doctor Watson has been dead for more than 100 years," Guy said, "and there's no going back."

"Why not? I've done it once already. "

"The only reason you're not being prosecuted is that I said I'd get you back to the U.S. I'm taking you to Traveler's Aid in Paris after we have dinner, and then you're in their hands."

"My cell phone?"

"Here it is. I charged it in my car."

"Thank you."

Cynthia went to the ladies' room for some privacy, and made one more call.

"Mom, it's Cynthia again. Please cancel your plans. Something important has come up, and I have to take care of it now. I'll call you again when I can."

With that, Cynthia swiped a roll of toilet paper and a bar of soap. Exiting the bathroom, she ran down the hallway toward the room she'd woken up in, followed by two guards and Guy Harrison, who yelled, "Cynthia! You'll go to jail this time! Stop!"

But Cynthia ran harder, leaped over the velvet ropes, and closed the door.

CHAPTER TEN

Cold early spring rain spattered against the windows of Cynthia's apartment, where she sat alone listening to it and drinking her second cold goblet of white wine.

The last few months had been a living hell. Not only did she have to face her parents from the inside of a jail cell after having vanished off the face of the earth for months, she soon realized that she couldn't tell anyone the full truth, despite the evidence in her camera and Professor Moriarty's voice: in this altered century, he was completely unknown, as was Sherlock Holmes. The only picture which would mean anything was that of Sir Christopher Kenyon.

"It's photoshopped," Cynthia's father said. "It has to be. There are times I'm ashamed of you, Cynthia."

"When would I have the chance?"

"For all anybody knows, you did all this in advance. Best hoax ever."

"Thanks, Dad. My number one supporter."

"Oh, don't say that, honey. This is one hard story to believe."

Once Cynthia returned to America, she found herself repeating a somewhat edited version of the truth, and now she was the unwilling darling of the paranormal believers, whom she regarded as downright crazy. A number of her friends dropped her, people she had never seen claimed to be lifelong buddies, and the magazine had replaced her long ago. Literary agents and movie producers swarmed like wasps, waving money and contracts for her story, but she turned them all down, and turned them down with finality. Now she was working under a slightly different name as a travel agent.

Not only that, but large parts of history had changed. World War I didn't begin with the assassination of the archduke Franz Ferdinand in Sarajevo; it began when Germany and Poland attacked Russia after the Bolshevik Revolution in 1917, and the war ran into the early 1920s. World War II followed on its heels with great speed, as a desperate Germany turned to Adolf Hitler sooner than Cynthia recalled from her history books, with hostilities breaking out in 1936, but ending in 1945 with the atomic attacks on the Japanese cities of Hiroshima and Nagasaki.

Closer to home, the Kenyon family had a very different history. In the new reality, Cynthia's paternal grandfather never served in World War II, and remarried after Cynthia's grandmother died giving birth to her Uncle Cyrus. The warm and loving woman who gave her free run of the farm in the summer never existed for Cynthia, a heartbreaking loss. The new reality created an entire branch of the family she had never met. A lot of the people who greeted Cynthia like lifelong friends on her return were perfect strangers, something she told them was due to "temporal amnesia."

Paul Hartke, at least, did not treat her like she was crazy. They had a number of long conversations, and during one, he explained his theory.

"I talked with Dr. April Cape at the Acoreus Museum, and to the young man who actually built the machine," Hartke told her." They're both astonished, and I think they're having a hard time believing it. Essentially, that kid found a way to capture light particles, put them in something he calls a 'quantum chamber' and use them to direct the machine through time. Revolutionary, really, and I can't wait to see it for myself."

"They still have it?"

"It seems so."

As if they'd let me anywhere near it, Cynthia thought.

"The time slip?"

"It's still my guess that the machine gives off some particle residue after it travels. Other particles would naturally be attracted, and you were close to the site of the last known one."

All this because John had to be a patriot, she thought, and sighed.

Even after all this time, Cynthia's heart pined for John Watson and it broke almost every time she thought how it all ended. She'd see his face when she closed her eyes, felt his touch in her dreams. She missed his passion, and she yearned to give him the children he so badly craved. She knew she had to find a way to go back, now that she knew it could be done. All she needed was to figure out how.

Cynthia had no idea how lonely she truly was until Leo Lawrence called from out of the blue and asked to meet her for lunch.

"Could it be someplace really quiet?" she asked. "Where nobody is a UFO nut?"

Leo seemed excited about something when he sat down opposite her in the quiet seafood restaurant, and it surprised Cynthia how happy she was to see him.

"I've been worried about you, but I've been too embarrassed to call," she said. "What happened after I left?"

"They sent in about a thousand cops, and the robbers had no chance. Nobody was hurt in the end, I got bruised up a little in the fight, but I'm okay now. But that's not what's important."

The waitress came with menus. Both ordered iced tea.

"I recommend the scallops," Leo said. "Anyway, I have what I hope is good news. We're related, you and I."

"Wait."

"What?"

"I need to know if your memories of how we met and what we talked about match mine. Please tell me."

The waitress arrived with iced tea for both of them, and Leo ran through the sequence of events: Watson's tin dispatch box, the discovery of Watson's notes for *The Hound of the Baskervilles,* finding the tickets inside, and the subsequent events.

"Thank God," Cynthia said with a sigh. "At least that much is right in the world."

"Anyway," Leo said, "I wondered how in the world my grandmother could even know about you, let alone get those tickets into that strongbox. So I climbed down the family tree."

"You found Sir Christopher, didn't you?"

Leo laughed.

"Yes, I did. He had a daughter with a mistress, and that daughter, it turns out, is one of my maternal great-great grandmothers. Lydia Parks was her name. Not only that, I've found all kinds of correspondence. She had quite a story to tell, did Lydia."

Lunch arrived, grilled halibut for Cynthia, and scallops for Leo, with side salads and more iced tea.

"She was involved with some private detective called Sherlock Holmes. Ever heard of him?"

Cynthia laughed.

"You have no idea," she said.

"It seems her husband James got mixed up with some jewel thieves, and he was acting as the middleman between the thieves and the fence. But the fence turned out to be Holmes, and he persuaded James to turn state's evidence. But here's the kicker: Holmes left her the strongbox when he died, and with the instructions that the box not leave the family's possession until it passed to you. He left precise dates, and this envelope."

Leo slid the envelope over. Inside, Cynthia found a photograph of herself and Watson and a note:

"My good Mrs. Parks,

"Please take the utmost care to ensure that this box and its contents not leave your family's possession until such time as it is to be opened by your descendant, Leo Lawrence, who will recognize the woman in the photograph. Please visit my solicitors at the earliest opportunity for your instructions and follow them to the letter.

"Gratefully yours,

"Sherlock Holmes"

"I can't believe this," Cynthia said. "I had no idea he had a sentimental streak."

"Who?"

"Sherlock Holmes," Cynthia said. "The man I knew had no use for the romantic side of life."

"Maybe he softened in his old age. I know he kept in touch with my great-grandmother for the longest time. He lived into his nineties."

Her eyes beginning to fill with tears, Cynthia knew what she had to do.

Making that appointment had to have been one of the most difficult tasks of her life, but Cynthia found herself across the desk of a scowling Dr. April Cape, director of the Acoreus' technology museum.

"Professor Hartke suggested I talk to you," Cynthia said. "He's quite impressed. He says you made a breakthrough."

Dr. Cape only glowered.

"It sure took some nerve for you to come back here," she said.

Now that she was closer to Dr. Cape than she was at the reception, Cynthia placed the woman's age at about 45, and it was clear that museum work not only paid well, but very well. Dr. Cape wore a well-tailored and perfectly coordinated cream-colored suit, and her shoes seemed to Cynthia to be beyond expensive. Her office was furnished with highly polished antiques and valuable modern art, her desk was covered with paperwork and magazines, and the window commanded a grand view of the museum grounds and the city below.

"We aren't entirely happy with the publicity your little stunt brought us," she said, "and, frankly, we'd have sued you if you had any money, which, by the look of things, you don't."

"I need your help," Cynthia said. "Where is the time machine now?"

"It's in storage, thanks to your vanishing act. I'm amazed the aliens didn't take it."

Cynthia could take no more. She tried to suppress the tears as they began to flow, but they would not be denied.

"Please at least pretend to take me seriously, Doctor Cape," she said as evenly as she could to conceal the pain and desperation so close to the surface. "I didn't volunteer for this!

The whole thing has made me look insane to people all over the world, I lost my job, my friends have dumped me and UFO geeks hit on my every time I go outside. I never wanted any of that! If I did, don't you think I'd be all over TV?"

Cynthia began to cry, and the physicist pushed a box of tissue over to her.

No chance now, she thought.

"Do you think I wanted to tell that idiotic story?" she continued. "But the truth would have gotten me put away!"

"I'm sorry," Dr. Cape replied, her tone softer, but still suspicious. "What can I do for you?"

"I have to go back," Cynthia said. "A lot of history changed while I was gone. I have to make it right."

"What are you saying?"

"That because of one brave act in 1887, the future of the world changes. I have to stop it. Think about it. What if my parents hadn't met as a result of my changing things?"

"The classic time paradox," Dr. Cape said. "If you go back in time and accidentally kill your grandfather you won't be born. But if you aren't born, you can't travel back to kill your grandfather, and so he lives. But if he does, you'll go back in time and kill him."

"Doctor Cape, what do you have to lose?" Cynthia said, trying not to beg. "If the machine doesn't work, then I won't go anywhere. Feel free to have a couple of guards there, put me in jail, I don't care. If I go and I'm successful, then history will be

82

restored and you can destroy that machine before someone else does real damage."

"In theory, you'll be setting yourself to run in this loop forever," Dr. Cape said. "The implications for the universe are profound. I can't let you do it, even if I believed you."

Cynthia slid a business card across the desk.

"Please call Dr. Hartke," she said. "He'll explain it."

"All right."

"Who designed the ship? Someone named Benson?"

"One of my graduate students, Roland Munson."

"Could I talk to him? Please?"

"I'll send him a text and see what he says."

Two days later, Cynthia sat at a wooden table across from a scrawny young long-haired man in his early 30s who wore an Einstein T-shirt and jeans, it being a sunny early May day. He, at least, was willing to listen. She sipped coffee while he spoke.

"I have read Moriarty's book, and it's brilliant," Munson said. "Way ahead of its time. The professor was dead by the time H.G. Wells wrote *The Time Machine*, but Wells wasn't a half-bad designer."

"So how did you make it work?"

"I have no idea why it did, and I'm speaking hypothetically here, because, let's face it Cynthia, your story is just a tad difficult to take at 100 percent face value. But, to greatly oversimplify, I modernized Wells' design to accommodate

Moriarty's river metaphor. I used the collector to gather light particles and agitate them to go faster, which is what breaks the time barrier."

Cynthia snorted.

"You took it for a test run," she said. "The machine was on when I dove into it. Don't deny it. You know I'm telling the truth. Where did you go?"

Munson blushed.

"I went back to the first World Science Fiction Convention at the New York World's Fair in 1939. I have pictures of myself with Isaac Asimov and Ray Bradbury when they were just teenagers. I made sure to keep my head down and my mouth shut, and I had a lot of fun."

"So why did I end up in London in 1882?"

"I wanted to meet Moriarty in person and let him know he was right. It would have been really cool to bring him back here to see the future. But one of the guards kicked me out while I was setting the navigator."

"Oh, thank God you didn't go!" Cynthia said. "Moriarty became a criminal mastermind. When I had the time slip, he was already planning to get it working."

"What?"

"It's a long story."

"You said time slip. Like the one at Versailles in 1901? Do you know that story?"

Cynthia nodded.

"Professor Hartke said it might be some sort of particle residue from the machine," Cynthia said.

Munson nodded and said, "That's as good a guess as any."

"This time I want to do it right," she said. "You'll help me?"

Munson nodded.

"I have some calculating to do," he said.

Cynthia knew what to pack in the suitcase this time: money, period appropriate clothing, a travel kit, moist towelettes, and travel food: in this case, mixed nuts, dried fruit, and bottled water.

Finding the money proved most difficult. Victorian-era British currency just couldn't be found at all, and the coins were ridiculously expensive – after all, they depended on the current price of gold, and even the least costly came in at around $30. Fortunately, lesser coins were easier to come by, but the whole adventure depleted what remaining cash she had.

What's the point in coming back? she thought.

Roland had a pass card to the museum, and no one bothered them as they took the freight elevator to the basement storage area.

"You're sure about the date?" he asked.

"It's got to be the first week in June, 1887 because the Jubilee takes place on June 20," Cynthia replied. "That should be plenty of time to stop the assassin and save the Queen."

Roland laughed.

"What?"

"That sounded so noble. I didn't think anyone other than Daniel Craig was allowed to say things like that."

As Cynthia felt herself vanishing into the time stream, she did not hear Roland's last words to her.

"Godspeed, Cynthia Kenyon," he said.

CHAPTER ELEVEN

The first thing Cynthia heard was a cry of shock.

"I'm so sorry, Mrs. Hudson!" Cynthia said as she emerged from the machine into a dimly lit basement, where Mrs. Hudson was rinsing laundry. "I didn't mean to startle you."

The older woman stared at Cynthia for a moment, and said, "It's Miss Kenyon, isn't it? Mr. Holmes' cousin?"

"That's right."

"Doctor Watson will be so relieved. He feared you were dead. He was inconsolable for weeks after you vanished."

"Is he in? I need to see them."

"Just as well you're here, Miss Kenyon. They're bickering again."

Cynthia felt for a light switch as they neared the top of the basement steps. That was one hard habit to break for someone from the era of electricity. Up the seventeen well-worn steps to Apartment B, where Cynthia heard the discussion through the door.

"Watson, when I agreed to let you write this study in scarlet, I had hoped you would simply place the facts of the case before the public and let my methods speak for themselves," Holmes was saying. "You're turning the thing into some sort of romantic thriller."

"Holmes, do you have any idea of why your own monographs generate so little interest except among specialists? It's because they're so dry. I would not be fair to the reader if I failed to convey the sense of adventure which made the case so noteworthy. Besides, am I not giving you half the earnings?"

Mrs. Hudson knocked gently.

"Not now, Mrs. Hudson! I told you we'd have the rent next week!" Holmes yelled through the door.

Mrs. Hudson opened the door anyway, and the sheer look of shock, mixed with joy, spread across Watson's face like an unexpected sunny break in the clouds on a stormy day.

Holmes dropped his cigarette, nonplussed possibly for the first time in his life.

"Miss Kenyon, I never expected the pleasure of seeing you again," he said.

"Shall I bring tea, Mr. Holmes?"

"What a delightful idea, Mrs. Hudson."

Holmes viewed her embrace with Watson with considerable distaste, and turned away when they kissed. At that moment, the original magic all seemed to return in a sudden wave, and she knew, in her heart, she had come home, to her proper place, the loving arms of Dr. John Watson.

"We had no idea what happened to you," Watson said once their embrace broke. "Where were you? It's been five years!"

"For me, it's been more like six months," Cynthia replied. "But I had to come back."

"Half the earnings, Watson?"

"Not the time, Holmes."

"Since it appears I shall be a lonely bachelor once again, I think I should address the practicalities."

"You have plenty to keep you busy, Holmes."

"I hope Mrs. Hudson returns in time to keep you two from consummating your reunion on the floor," Holmes grumbled.

Once the tea was poured and the door closed, Holmes said, "Your last visit, I take it, had consequences beyond what you expected, for you would otherwise not be here now."

Cynthia nodded.

"I had to," she said. "Otherwise, John dies in two weeks."

Watson almost dropped his cup.

"What?"

"There's going to be an assassination attempt on the Queen at the Golden Jubilee," Cynthia said. "John's going to be in the crowd at Windsor Station, and he'll take the bullet intended for her. And because of that, no one will remember Sherlock Holmes, and because of that, history changes."

"What?" Holmes asked.

"I know I'm not supposed to tell you these things, but I don't care. I don't care if it causes a time paradox. I can't let you die!"

"Cynthia, what about the Queen? Surely I must put my unworthy life before Her Majesty's."

"It's not unworthy to me!"

"Watson, the Jubilee is more than two weeks away." Holmes said. "Can you tell me the circumstances?"

Cynthia related the results of her Internet searches, and handed Holmes printouts of contemporary news accounts.

"Hmm. No coroner's report, apparently. So you don't know where Watson was standing? The name of the assassin? I know it would be too much to ask about the angle of the bullet or which direction it came from."

"I'm a travel agent, not a detective."

"Holmes, how often have I seen you fill that ghastly needle when you're bored? This is a challenge you'll never see again."

"True. Still, I wish you had learned more, cousin."

"I also wanted to find that lost family member while I'm here. Could you help me with that?"

Holmes nodded.

"It's time to put my ear on the rail track," he said, rising. "I'm off to Pall Mall. Will you join us for dinner, Miss Kenyon?"

"Of course."

"Splendid. The Blue Posts at seven, then. Miss Kenyon, I must say it is a delight to see you again."

Watson's face radiated with a devilish smile.

Rarely had Cynthia experienced lovemaking so vigorous, and by the time they were done she just wanted to sleep.

"Cynthia, I can't bear to lose you again."

"I know, John. I've made my mind up. I'm staying after I've done my piece for history. If anything else changes, I don't want to know about it. And you'll have so many stories to tell. All I have to do is stay out of history's way."

"I've had other romances since you left, but none compare to you," Watson said. "You've made me a very happy man today, my darling."

Cynthia sighed and nestled in his arms, safe and secure.

For the next several days, Sherlock Holmes seldom showed his face after breakfast, which suited Cynthia just fine. She enjoyed having Watson to herself, and she even began to accompany him on his rounds, occasionally acting as his nurse. She learned bandages, how to stop bleeding, learned, to her amazement, that cocaine acts as a local anesthetic, and she learned how to give injections.

"You're quite remarkable," Watson said at one point. "Most women would be quite fainthearted just by the sight of blood."

"You're going to have to learn to stop talking like that if we're going to be married," Cynthia replied. "Female doctors are common in my time, and I've seen far worse things in horror movies."

"You'll have to show me a movie sometime so I'll know what it is."

"I should be able to do that in twenty years or so."

Watson laughed.

"What will we tell our children about the future?" he asked.

"That's really important to you, isn't it?"

"I lost my parents years ago, and my brother was a hopeless drunkard who somehow got kicked in the head by a horse, which had the merciful quality of killing him instantly. I saw all the bloodshed I care to in Afghanistan. On more than one occasion, I had to tell a wounded soldier there was no hope, and see the anguish in his eyes, and I've seen men die suddenly before I could aid them. I want life, Cynthia. More than anything, I want a legacy for my son."

"Or daughter."

"Yes. I keep forgetting that. Do women carry the family name in the future?"

"If they want to. It's a matter of choice."

When they returned to Baker Street, they found Sherlock Holmes in his mouse-grey dressing gown and armchair, smoking a pipe and sipping whiskey, something he seldom did during the day. Cynthia immediately opened the window.

"If I told you what I know about tobacco, you two would quit tomorrow."

"Then don't tell me," Holmes said. "Miss Kenyon, are you certain there will be an assassination attempt on the day of the Queen's Golden Jubilee?"

"I am."

"Tell me, was the assassin ever caught?"

"No, not even identified."

"Then a far more sinister plot is afoot than I first feared, or, worse, just one deranged man lurking in the bushes somewhere. My investigations have provided little evidence of any organized plan, but I have fully alerted Scotland Yard to the possibility. In any event, Watson, I must insist you not go to Windsor station that day."

"But the Queen, Holmes!"

"She will be amply protected, I assure you. I have certain friends in Her Majesty's government, and I have briefed them with what little I know."

"There are still a few days to go," Cynthia said. "Your luck will change."

"As it happens, yours already has, if you and Watson have nothing to do tomorrow."

Holmes reached into the pocket of his dressing gown and produced a pair of tickets, handing them to Watson.

"Holmes, this is uncommonly generous!" Watson said.

"Nonsense. I thought our guest would like to see a little bit of home."

"John, what are they?"

"Two tickets to Buffalo Bill's Wild West Show. They're part of the American Exhibition. I keep meaning to take you, but these tickets are terribly difficult to come by. How did you do it, Holmes?"

"I solved a little problem for Mr. Cody not so long ago," he replied. "He was most grateful."

That day proved to be one of the happiest days of Cynthia's life.

"Holmes knows I've been dying to go," Watson said. "I've never seen genuine red savages before."

"John, there's something else you should know about my time," Cynthia said. "We don't talk about people that way anymore. I know there's nothing I can do about the attitudes here, and I have held my tongue so often it sometimes hurts. But we've been striving for racial equality in America for generations. White people regularly vote for black candidates, and the terrible things we did to the Indians shame us now. Or I should say, will shame us in the future."

"Don't worry, then," Watson said, with a disappointed sigh. "I'll just take Holmes. I didn't know it would upset you."

"I didn't say that I don't want to go, but just understand that white supremacy is frowned upon in my time. We don't accept it anymore."

"I'll just give the tickets to one of my patients, and you need not worry."

"No! I've been hearing about Buffalo Bill all my life, and a chance to see Anne Oakley in person? I can't turn that down. It's just that I thought you should know the context, is all."

Cynthia hadn't seen a crowd so enthused even at pricy rock concerts.

"It looks like all of London's here," Watson said.

"John, look! Popcorn!"

The popcorn brought back any number of memories for Cynthia, but she found the flavor of 19th century popcorn to be heavenly. The popcorn of 1887 had fuller flavor, and benefited greatly from not being popped in palm oil. Even the salt seemed more flavorful somehow.

"You shouldn't have had me buy this," Watson said as they made their way front of the crowd. "This is delicious. I could stuff myself on it. Here, find us something to drink, will you?"

Cynthia returned with root beer, which Watson had never tasted and found delicious. For Cynthia, the beverage was a revelation: no artificial coloring or high fructose corn syrup, but instead, she detected coriander, licorice, juniper, and wintergreen, among others mixed together in a robust brew that put its 21st century corporate counterparts to shame.

"You're going to turn me into a fat man if we keep this up," Watson said.

"Look! There's Buffalo Bill!"

Cynthia took her cell phone out and filmed much of the opening parade, led by the tall mustachioed man in the saddle wearing buckskins, Buffalo Bill himself. He led cowboys, Indians, Mexicans, stunt riders, genuine bison, cattle, elk, people dressed as pioneers.

"What are you doing?" Watson asked.

"I'll show you when we get home," she said.

The crowd thrilled to the full scale attack on a stagecoach, the Indians in full battle regalia, the riding and roping demonstrations, but the moment Cynthia wanted seemed a long time in coming. Finally, Annie Oakley stepped into the arena.

"I had no idea she was so beautiful," Cynthia said.

Oakley, in full cowgirl costume, blew kisses to the crowd, and Cynthia felt a pang of jealousy looking at the admiration in Watson's eyes. She was about Cynthia's age, with long, dark hair worn just past shoulder length. Whether she knew it or not, Oakley had an undeniable air of sexiness about her that somehow made her marksmanship more remarkable. She had the crowd in the palm of her hand.

Her husband, Frank Butler, a man a few years older than she, tossed a glass sphere into the air, which she blasted with ease. Two, then three, and up to six, to the crowd's delight. She put a hole right in the centers of coins tossed in the air, and then came the trick that had the crowd holding its breath.

Butler held a playing card up for his wife to hit. One shot later, a clean hole in the center. Then Butler turned the card sideways. Not one sound could be heard, and then CRACK!

Annie Oakley split the card in half.

"And I've got it all on video!" Cynthia cried.

After they returned to Baker Street, Cynthia said, "John, you wanted to see a movie?"

"I thought you said it wouldn't be for another twenty years."

"I have a sample for you."

Watson's eyes glowed with wonder as he relived the spectacle again, and he said, "Holmes, you have to see this!"

"What a remarkable device this is," Holmes said after his viewing. "I know of experiments being done with moving pictures, but this is quite sophisticated. You live in marvelous times, Miss Kenyon."

"So do you, Mr. Holmes."

CHAPTER TWELVE

On the morning of June 20, Sherlock Holmes sat down to breakfast and said, "If there is any organized plot to assassinate the Queen, I have been unable to discern it."

"Then it must be some random madman," Watson said. "I wish I knew what to do."

"Your staying alive is the way history is meant to be, John," Cynthia said. "All you have to do is stay away from Windsor station. It can't be that difficult. You can see the Queen during her procession tomorrow."

"Watson, no need to trouble yourself," Holmes said. "I shall take my binoculars to Windsor station and wait. We know something the assassin doesn't: the very minute he plans to make his move. I will ensure that he does not."

"That's settled," Cynthia said.

Three sudden, urgent knocks prompted Watson over to the door, and a young woman looked at him with pleading eyes.

"Are you a doctor?" she asked.

"Yes."

"Come quickly, please, and bring your nurse. There's a woman giving birth in the carriage!"

"I'm coming, too," Cynthia said.

"Yes, you should learn about midwifery," Watson said.

A growler waited at the end of the street.

"The patient is in there," the young woman said.

"It'll have to do," Watson said.

The young woman opened the door, and Cynthia heard someone say, "Send in the nurse first."

"Cynthia, please make sure the patient is suitably comfortable."

Cynthia entered the carriage, followed by the young woman who closed the door, and the carriage immediately clattered off. Cynthia did not see any woman in labor, just a workman sitting opposite her.

"What is—"

"Hello, miss. Never thought I'd see you again."

The rough named Harry from Cynthia's first encounter sat across from her, holding a heavy revolver.

"Professor Moriarty's been looking for you," he said. "Ruth, blindfold her."

The blindfold came off to reveal a pleasant parlor, tea and sandwiches, two large, rough-looking men, and the reptilian Professor James Moriarty, who glowered with suspicion.

"I never thought our paths would cross again," he said. "You can only imagine how pleased I was to see your nuptials announced in the *Telegraph*."

"Professor, I really can't help you," Cynthia said. "I'm not a physicist and I'm not an engineer."

"One of the greatest inventions in history has been gathering dust in a warehouse for years," Moriarty said. "Your presence here can only be explained by one thing: you must know how to make that machine work. You will show me tonight. I have one or two other matters requiring my attention. In the meantime, you may ponder your fate: a happy marriage to the good Doctor Watson, or enforced employment in a brothel. It's up to you. Don't let her out of your sight."

"We could prepare her, Professor."

"She is not to be touched without my permission. I hope I have made that clear."

With that, Moriarty left the room.

"This is ridiculous," Cynthia said. "It's the simplest thing. I could even show you monkeys how to do it. It's got to be here in the building, right?"

"Miss, you're not leaving this room until the Professor gets back."

Cynthia sighed, and found a book. Moriarty returned in time for afternoon tea.

"First, I want you to tell me how you escaped five years ago," he said.

"You explained it yourself, Professor. I experienced a time slip. It seems that part of France is an area where time is sort of a pool in the river. I had that experience due to some sort of temporal residue from the machine. At least that's how it was explained to me."

"Because you had already traveled before, it was easier for you to travel again, is that it?'

"I didn't intend for that to happen."

Moriarty snorted, turned to one of his men and said, "Let's go to the machine."

Again, Cynthia was blindfolded and taken in a carriage, this time to a large, shabby warehouse on the Thames. She thought of making a break for it, diving into the river, and swimming for her life, but Moriarty no doubt had anticipated something like that, because the two guards kept closer to her sides than ever.

Once inside, Cynthia was astonished to see the large space illuminated by electric light, and she saw neatly organized rows in a space she guessed might have been half the length of a football field. Moriarty led the way down one of those rows, and stopped about halfway down.

"That one," he said, pointing to a large pine crate.

The two men had a surprisingly easy time getting the crate onto the wooden floor; they climbed stepladders and opened it quickly. One's face went white.

"Professor," he said, "it's not here."

"What?"

Moriarty climbed up one of the stepladders and peered into the crate.

"You had something to do with this!" he yelled at Cynthia.

"Me? I had no idea this place even existed."

Moriarty's face softened to a scowl.

"No, you couldn't, could you? Perhaps your meddlesome friend Sherlock Holmes is responsible. I wonder what he would do to win your freedom. Hand over your cell phone."

Cynthia retrieved the device from her hidden pocket and turned it on.

"Jenkins, Benton, hold her. Benton, cover her mouth with your hand."

Moriarty took a photo.

"Here's a pound," the professor said to Jenkins. "Get a street urchin to take the device to this address when you can, and to make sure to tell the recipient to wait for further instructions."

CHAPTER THIRTEEN

A distinct chill in the air awakened Cynthia, and she awoke to a cold and empty house. Finding a shawl in the dresser, she looked all through the house, but found no one. The colorful trees in the twilight outside told her autumn had arrived, and she realized she had traveled again.

Oh, my God, she thought, *when am I?*

Peering outside, she saw a bustling busy street, but the people there clearly were not the middle class of London she was accustomed to: their clothing looked cheap, the streets were dirtier, the language much rougher, and the women more poorly dressed. Many of them had been drinking, and drinking heavily, to judge from their staggering gaits, all pointed to a different part of London. Cynthia began to think she would not be safe if she stayed here.

But at the moment, she had little choice. There was enough wood for a fire, and newspapers to light it; the paper on top of the pile was dated August 4, 1888, so she had gone ahead by about a year. Once she had a good fire going, she huddled under some blankets on a sofa and tried to get back to sleep, an effort which proved futile.

Peering out the window hours later, she saw the streets all but deserted.

This is as good a time as any, Cynthia thought, especially after finding no food in the pantry. She scoured the bedrooms for money, unearthing some coins which she hoped would be enough for a cab ride to Baker Street and something to eat. Dressing as warmly as she could, Cynthia stepped into the cold darkness and began to walk.

Cynthia spotted gaslight in some of the windows as the area began to stir for the new morning. Horses began to clip-clop by, and it would not be long, she hoped, before some shops opened. A street sign told her she had come to Whitechapel High Street, which looked like a main thoroughfare. She decided she would walk to the east, into the awakening dawn, but after a few steps, she felt something wrong.

Am I being followed?

Once planted, the seed began to grow. Cynthia's heart began to beat a little faster as she walked, eyeing the down-at-their-heels denizens of the area with greater and greater suspicion. Some of them openly appraised her, and when they tried to talk to her, she walked faster, wishing for the entire world she had remembered to bring along pepper spray. Once she reached a place called Mitre Square, the suspicion became a reality as a short man with red hair, equally red moustache, wearing a bowler hat and a frock coat approached her.

"Good morning, miss," he said. "Bit dangerous for a lady like yourself to be walking around alone."

"I'm fine, thank you. I'm just looking for a cab stand."

"There's one at the end of the alley, miss," he said. "It's on my way. I'll join you."

Cynthia did not like his look at all; the man had an air about him which set off all her alarms, and she thought of what might happen if she ran. But that might set him off. Fearing she had made a mistake, she let him accompany her.

"What's your name?" he asked.

"Cynthia. What's yours?"

Cynthia saw some metal glint as he replied, "They call me Jack."

The blade sunk into her chest before she could move, and a foul, dirty hand covered her mouth before she could scream. The burning agonies of hell raced through her body even as a feeling of cold began to set in. Jack started to slash and rip the knife through her flesh, the blood spurted high, and a dazed Cynthia dropped to the filthy alley floor, Jack and his knife looming over her, the blade descending again, her life about to end in a squalid alleyway in Whitechapel under the vicious, unforgiving knife of Jack the Ripper.

"You there!" a familiar voice cried.

Suddenly the knife came free and Jack vanished down the alley and into the next street, even as Sherlock Holmes and Dr. John Watson ran to her.

"Cynthia!"

Holmes pulled a police whistle from his pocket and blew it, the high harsh trill echoing in the filthy alley.

"What … are …"

"Don't talk," Watson said in a calm, soothing tone. "It's John. It's all right. Right now, you are going into shock. I am going to do a few things to stem the bleeding, but they will be very painful. Bite down on this piece of rubber. Concentrate on that."

Cynthia could not stifle the cries of agony as she felt Watson's fingers and instruments at work. Sometimes her body rebelled, involuntarily writhing when she discovered a whole new world of bright, jagged pain. But at last the new pain began to subside, and Cynthia's eyes closed as she began to lose consciousness.

Two bobbies raced into the alleyway.

"No ether, Watson?"

"No time to let it start working. Not the best operating theatre, Holmes."

"The Ripper," Holmes said. "This woman is still alive. She's seen him! Get an ambulance!"

"Blimey," said one of the cops as the other ran, only to vomit at the end of the alley.

"My machine," Cynthia hissed. "Is it—"

"Yes, still in Mrs. Hudson's cellar. Don't talk. Everything will be all right."

But soon Cynthia lost consciousness. When her eyes opened, the welcome sight of Watson almost gave her hope, but the expression on his face told her everything.

"I've lost too much blood." Just getting the words out took an effort. "I'm going to die, John."

"Not if I have anything to say about it."

"Get me to the time machine," she said, fainting again.

Cynthia tried to open her eyes, but couldn't. She had the sensation of being moved.

"Holmes, are you sure?" she heard Watson say.

"Watson, you said you hadn't seen wounds that bad since Maiwand. If there's to be any hope of saving her life, she has to go to her own time."

"Then I'm going with her."

"You can't, Watson. Just write some instructions for her doctors. It's her only chance."

"Holmes, I have to know!"

She had the sensation of being lain down on the leather seat of the time machine, and she heard someone manipulating the controls, even as Watson's lips, his love and human warmth, caressed Cynthia's own.

"I have to believe the medicine of the 21st century can save you," he whispered. "Come back to me, my darling. Come back to me."

"Watson, I'm shocked. What about Miss Mor--"

"Chide me later!" Watson barked. "I certainly hope you know what you're doing."

"So do I," Holmes said, and Cynthia fainted again. She did not hear Holmes' fingers as he tapped the keys, or see him set the destination with the skill and precision of the machine's inventor. Nor did she see the anxious looks on both their faces as she disappeared into the void of time.

Once again, that strange and unique moving sensation, and a gasp from people in the gallery.

"That woman!"

"Where did she come from?"

"Look at all that blood!"

"Call 911!"

"John ..." she whispered.

Blackness again.

When Cynthia first came back to consciousness, she felt the anesthetic buzzing in her head, and saw her parents' faces, and someone unknown, looking down on her.

"Cynthia," her anxious mother said, "Can you hear me? Do you know who I am?"

"Scarecrow, and the Lion, and Auntie Em," Cynthia said with a weak laugh. "There's no place like home."

She went back to sleep.

When Cynthia next regained consciousness, she still felt weak, but also much better and somewhat in control. Someone who looked like a refugee from Buffalo Bill's Wild West show looked down at her, but he wore a white coat and had a stethoscope hanging from his neck.

"Good morning, Ms. Kenyon," he said. "You gave us quite a fright."

"Where am I?"

"City Central Hospital, about a mile from the museum where you were attacked. I have to say, the circumstances are strange."

"Who are you?"

"I'm Doctor Blackfeather. I'm the one who patched you back together. I don't know where you were before, but they should be closed down. Whoever wrote that note had atrocious handwriting, to say the least. You were developing infections, and some internal organs had been badly punctured. But whoever wrote that note knew an awful lot about internal medicine. What I don't understand is why he dated it 1888."

"Because it was 1888, Doctor."

"And I suppose you were attacked by Jack the Ripper."

"I was, but Sherlock Holmes chased him off and got me to a hospital."

Dr. Blackfeather laughed.

"Still a little woozy, I see. Perfectly all right, it's to be expected. Be sure to take some solid food if you feel up to it. You've been on an IV tube for days."

"Thank you for saving my life," she said.

"We saved the baby, too."

"What?"

"You didn't know? You certainly would have in another few weeks."

"Poor John," Cynthia said. "He'll never know."

"Is he the father? Aren't you going to tell him?"

"I can't. By now, he'll have been dead for about ninety years."

"You aren't telling me that time machine in the museum actually works, are you?"

"It really does."

Dr. Blackfeather just smiled.

So many unanswered questions. Her cell phone, long since gone, and all she had to support the truth was Watson's note, dated October 25, 1888, something Dr. Blackfeather assumed was part of an intricate hoax to cash in on the publicity.

The number of visitors overwhelmed Cynthia at first. Several reporters had called, but all she could say to them was that she was too weak to talk, except to say that her condition had been downgraded from critical, and she would soon be receiving physical therapy.

Her parents proved all but unendurable.

"How can you expect us to believe a story like that?" her father demanded. "You stayed with Sherlock Holmes? Who else did you meet? Hercule Poirot? Sam Spade?"

"Dad, you can believe what you want, but I don't care. Anyway, I'm having Watson's baby."

Now her mother guffawed.

"I hope he doesn't turn out like Nigel Bruce," she said.

"I asked Doctor Blackfeather to give me the note they found when I came back."

"This was written by a doctor, all right," her father said.

"The date."

"Is some sort of hoax you've cooked up for the Internet?"

"Dad, I'm having the child by a man who was born in 1852! Why would I make that up? Talk to Roland Munson at the Acoreus. He built the thing."

"Lewis, she believes it."

"I think it's the painkillers," said Lewis Kenyon. "Let's go, Veronica. Maybe after she's had more time to recover."

Next came a social worker from the police.

"I'm here to make sure you're all right and to get a statement if you feel up to it," the woman said.

"My own parents don't believe me," she said. "Why should you?"

"Ms. Kenyon, if we don't know who attacked you, he could kill again."

Cynthia laughed and said, "He's been dead for more than 100 years."

Finally, two people Cynthia actually wanted to see: Leo Lawrence and Roland Munson. Leo, she saw, had Watson's tin dispatch box under his arm.

"Thank God you're all right," Roland said, handing her some cold water. "I've been wanting to meet you."

"You don't know—no, I guess you wouldn't, would you? I'm Cynthia Kenyon, Roland. You wouldn't recall our last meeting. It was long ago and far away."

"Cynthia," said Leo, "what are you talking about?"

"Later, Leo. The doctor tells me I'm going to be here for a few weeks, and I'm pregnant."

The men exchanged looks.

"It's Doctor Watson's," she said.

"You wouldn't believe how hot you are right now," Roland said.

"What? That's your idea of—"

"I meant hot property, as in viral. Somebody in the museum was shooting video of the time machine, and you just appear out of nowhere, and the machine seemed to glow. That got onto the Internet, and now everybody wants to know what happened. Ever since they found out I built the thing, the phone hasn't stopped ringing. We had to take it off display again."

"How long have I been gone?"

"About a year or so."

"Great."

"Cynthia, I found a few more things in the box that I think you ought to see."

Leo placed the box on a dresser and took some items from it.

"Here's a letter for you from none other than John H. Watson, M.D.," he said. "There's also this."

"My cell phone!"

"I charged it for you. I hope it still works."

Cynthia let out a cry of joy at seeing the pictures again, especially the excellent shot of Buffalo Bill Cody on his horse.

"Tell them I faked this!" she cried as she showed her guests the video. She pressed a few more buttons and handed it to Leo.

"That looks like Chief Sitting Bull," he said. "Really?"

Smiling, Cynthia nodded.

"You saw that show?" Roland asked. "What was it like?"

"Spectacular," she said. "I'm going to have to write this down someday."

"Well, we won't keep you," Leo said. "I'm sure you need your rest."

"Roland, wait. One thing. At one point Professor Moriarty had possession of the machine, and he had it crated up. But when they opened the crate the machine was gone."

"Of course it was," Roland said. "I only built the one machine. Even with time travel, you can only be in one place at a time. So when you went back, the machine changed locations."

113

"So where did the one on display come from?"

"It's the same machine. It vanished when you arrived."

Cynthia yawned.

"Come back again," she said. "I have a lot to tell you. Especially you, Roland."

CHAPTER FOURTEEN

Transcribed from a recording found on Cynthia Kenyon's cell phone, per Leo Lawrence:

For Miss Cynthia Kenyon:

Though our paths have crossed for the last time, there are still a few loose bows to tie. First, thank you for your observations of the Ripper, particularly the description. I can only imagine how painful reliving the experience must have been, but you provided invaluable information which might have changed everything were I able to act on it in time.

Watson, bless his heart, chides me for being a fussbudget, but some things remain, and only you can handle them. I found the recording in which you explained the time machine to Professor Moriarty, and used the information to learn the machine myself. The password, by the way, is "underpaid." I confess I gave it a try, and met Mr. Munson, the young man who invented the thing. I made him promise to keep my visit an absolute secret, for nothing less would do. I told him to expect your arrival, and instructed him to send two things back to me in 1888: a photograph of Watson's child, if any, and what you remember of your encounter with Jack the Ripper. That information led me to him, but by then it was too late. He somehow found I had caught his scent, and he threw himself into the Thames. I have kept his identity hidden for the sake of his family; there is no need to punish them for his wretched and cowardly actions. I may make arrangements to reveal the details long after my own death.

After you left, Watson was despondent for days. He had diagnosed your pregnancy. Had the fetus been better developed, it, too, might have fallen to the Ripper's blade.

I advise destroying the time machine after its final use. In the end, no good can come from it. I am grateful to have met you and for our adventures together, but we are all the creatures of our times, and I believe Providence intended it to be so. May you enjoy all the blessings the future seems to promise.

I am,
Your eternal friend,
Sherlock Holmes

***

221B Baker Street
December 25, 1889

Dearest Cynthia,

Given the blessings which have enriched my life since we last met, I feel Christmas is the perfect day for me to write this missive. My wife and I are in Baker Street to pay Holmes the compliments of the season and share a bit of Christmas cheer. I

116

write knowing you will never again respond, but I feel I must tell you the aftermath of your adventure and to thank you for the photograph. I enclose a copy so you'll know which one to send, and wrote the date on which you sent it on the reverse. I understand why you never came back. I was engaged to Miss Mary Morstan when we last met, but under the circumstances I felt it best to keep that information to myself in order to give you hope.

I pray young John is thriving, as I'm sure he must be in the remarkable world in which you live. I only wish I could have joined you somehow and raised a proper family, but I'm sure my medical knowledge is so ancient and primitive by your society's standards I could never hold my own, and medicine is the only career I ever wanted.

When the photograph arrived, it settled my greatest fear. I was overjoyed to learn you had survived that monster we now call Jack the Ripper. You are, I believe, the sole survivor, and Holmes is dying for your insights into such monstrous villainy. For one thing, you could give us an accurate description, and for another, you have looked evil in the eye and seen its soul. The Ripper, to this day, has never been caught, and if Holmes knows who it is, he won't tell me for his own peculiar reasons. One thing is certain: after Holmes read of a certain suicide in the papers and viewed the body, he made his conclusions clear to Scotland Yard, and they stopped searching. That happened about a month after his last, and most ghastly, attack.

Thanks to your information, Holmes was able to detect the would-be assassin of Queen Victoria at the Golden Jubilee. He simply placed himself in the assassin's shoes, and pondered where the safest place could be to fire a single fatal shot. He went to that location two hours before the Queen's train arrived and waited. The man turned out to be an Irish rebel named Brendan O'Connor, but Holmes disarmed him easily and turned him over to Inspector Lestrade. The public never knew.

As to your last situation, I feared for your life once we brought you to Baker Street. I have seen wounds similar to yours inflicted during combat, and wrote a long note detailing the locations of the wounds, the organs they affected, and my assessment of the damage done. I used some techniques I improvised in the heat of battle to close your wounds as best I could, but you had lost so much blood, my own prognosis was most grim.

Holmes had learned to operate your remarkable machine. My most fervent prayer was that he knew what he was doing, but the child who brought your cell phone to us left it behind, and Holmes put what he had learned from it to good use. All I remember is his pressing some buttons, punching some numbers on that most unusual typewriter, and pushing a lever. He then stepped back, and you simply vanished. Only in the works of Jules Verne did I suspect such was possible.

I thank you for your decision to name our child after me. I only wish I could be present when he encounters some of my descendants. Perhaps you'll visit once again in that amazing machine and we'll talk once more.

Wishing you the compliments of the season, I remain,
Your loving friend,
John H. Watson, M.D.

AFTERWORD

First, apologies to all my outraged Sherlockian friends, who are no doubt appalled that I have written this tale. However, it is not always the author's choice. I conceived the basic story a few years ago, and it kept percolating until it was ready to come out. Besides, we live in the era of wildly different Sherlocks in the forms of Robert Downey, Jr., Benedict Cumberbatch and Jonny Lee Miller, excellent interpretations all, and none of which dull the luster of the original. I doubt I can do him any harm.

But even though I chose science fiction for this particular story, I have rooted as much of it as I can in the genuine. Alexandra Park, Jack the Ripper, and the Versailles time slip were all real, or nearly so. What I really wanted to do was give Dr. Watson more of a role.

Far too many people assume Watson's sole role is to be the readers' viewpoint and the lens through which we see Holmes' brilliance. But Watson was much more than that. He'd had a pretty exciting life before meeting Sherlock Holmes, and an experience of women on three continents: Europe and Asia, certainly, and the other one, likely, was America. That, at least, is suggested by the justly unperformed play by Conan Doyle, *Angels of Darkness.* That's the Watson I felt should have some more exposure.

I also wanted to explore Lestrade a little more. In the Canon, he is nothing more than Holmes' unworthy sparring partner, but he did hold the rank of Inspector and on the force, anyway, deserved some respect. We may not have seen the last of him in my stories.

Alexandra Park was a genuine race course, and Watson's penchant for the ponies is well known. So is the fact that he married at least twice. I cannot believe Watson was any sort of Victorian prude when it came to sex, and let's face it, under the surface of all that stuffy morality, an awful lot of people were sinning. Watson was certainly attracted to, and attracted by, women. I thought he'd waited long enough.

I base my description of Jack on that of Joseph Lawende, who saw a man and woman on the way to Mitre Square, ten minutes before Catherine Eddowes was found on Sept. 30, 1888. I base Holmes' conclusions on the case of Montague John Druitt, one of the five possible suspects named by Sir Melville Macnaghten in his famous memorandum. For some reason, Scotland Yard's hunt for the Ripper dropped off considerably after Druitt's suicide by drowning in the Thames. This doesn't mean he was necessarily the Ripper, of course, but it does mean he was under suspicion.

The Versailles time slip comes from the story of Charlotte Moberly and Eleanor Jourdain, who toured the gardens of Versailles on August 10, 1901. You could not encounter two women less likely to hallucinate, see little green men or try to pull off a hoax. At the time, Moberly served as president of St. Hugh's College in Oxford, and Jourdain was her assistant. She went on to a distinguished academic career of her own.

Off in search of Marie Antionette's private residence, the Petite Trianon, they encountered people in period dress, yet they had a flat, unnatural quality, as if frozen in time. They encountered others, and asked another man in period costume for directions, which he gave. They crossed a bridge, and encountered a woman who, for all they knew, was Marie Antionette. They returned to Versailles, but the day lingered, and eventually they tried to authenticate their experiences, documented in a book titled, *An Adventure,* published under pseudonyms in 1911.

If you have made it this far, I thank you for your patience.

Stephen Seitz
Springfield, Vt.

Also from MX Publishing

Visit www.mxpublishing.com for dozens of other Sherlock Holmes novels, novellas, short story collections, Conan Doyle biographies, Holmes travel books and more.

MX Publishing is the award-winning world's largest independent Sherlock Holmes Book publishers with over 50 new authors and 100 new Sherlock Holmes stories in print.

Sherlock Holmes – Studies in Legacy.
The Untold Adventures of Sherlock Holmes Volume 2

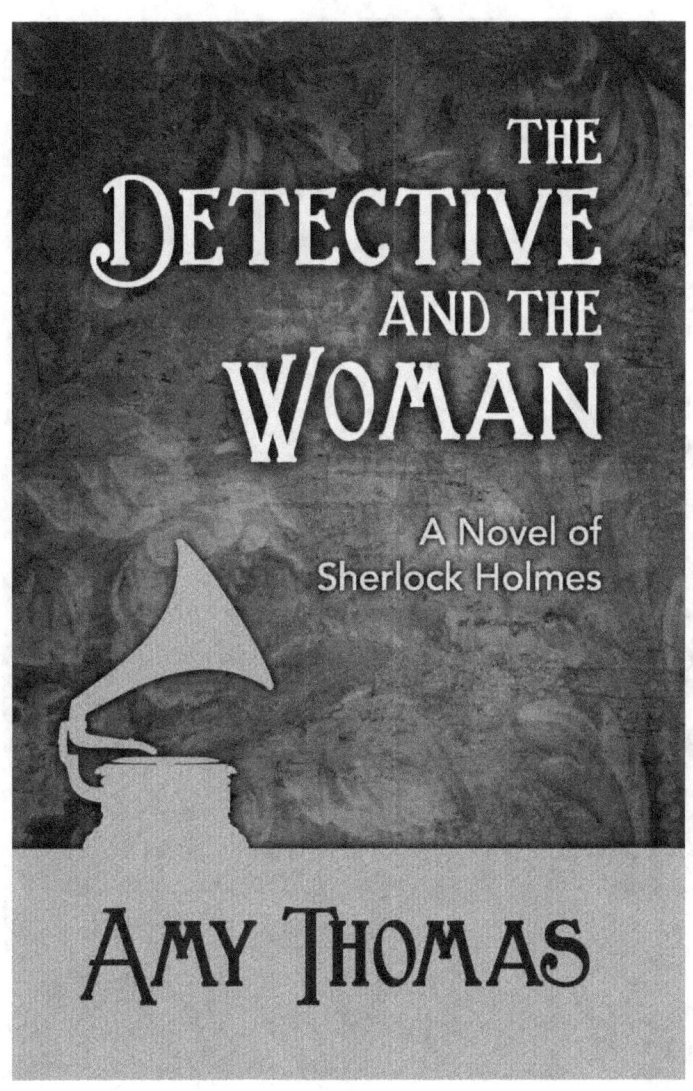

The Detective and The Woman and the new sequel, The Detective
The Woman and The Winking Tree

BENEDICT CUMBERBATCH

In Transition

Lynnette Porter

AN UNAUTHORISED PERFORMANCE BIOGRAPHY

Benedict Cumberbatch, In Transition
The definitive performance biography.

The Art of Deduction
A collection of fan art and stories celebrating BBC Sherlock
All royalties go to Help For Heroes

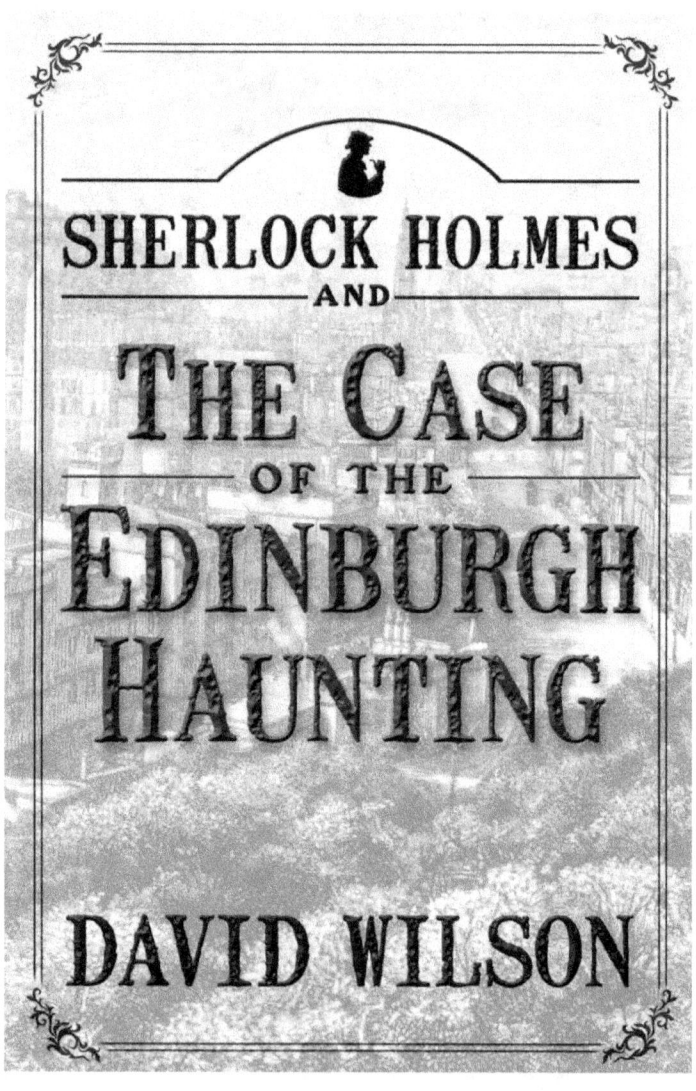

SHERLOCK HOLMES
AND

THE CASE
OF THE
EDINBURGH
HAUNTING

DAVID WILSON

A traditional Holmes story set in Scotland.

Holmes and Watson are sent to Russia on their most dangerous
mission ever.

The first of three Holmes military novels from war veteran Kieran
McMullen.

Traditional Holmes from Tim Symonds. The sequel is called
Sherlock Holmes and The Case of The Bulgarian Codex.

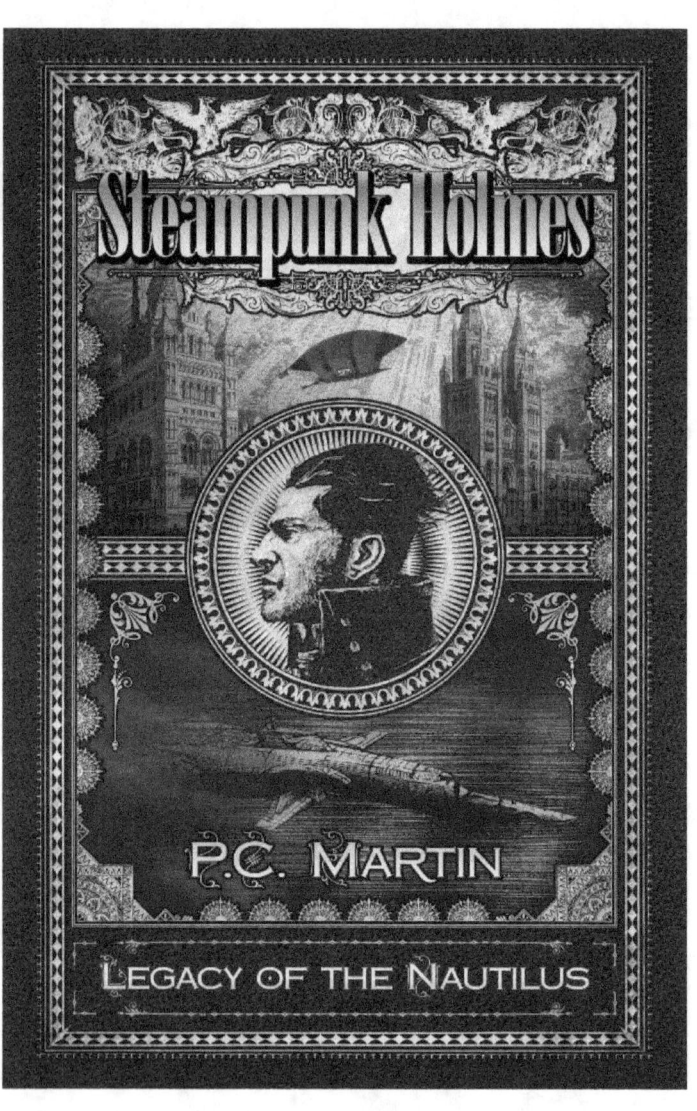

Steampunk Holmes

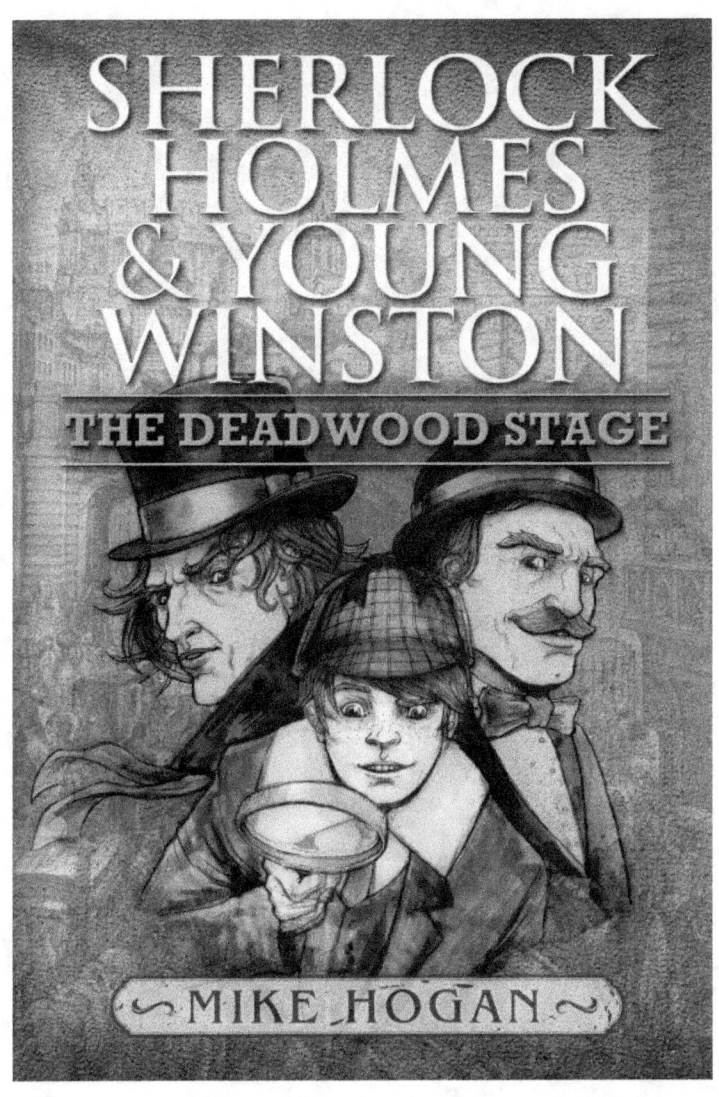

Sherlock Holmes and Young Winston – The Deadwood Stage.

The first in the acclaimed trilogy from Mike Hogan.

www.ingramcontent.com/pod-product-compliance
Lightning Source LLC
Chambersburg PA
CBHW071314130626
46556CB00004B/1610